He s⋯   .

"Wow," tł⋯   r

as she snuggled agaïıͳͳ ⋯   n

the aftermath.

"I hear bells," she said.

"Honey, I hear bells, too. I think it's your phone."

His cell phone rang and they pulled back to look at each other.

"This can't be good news." He kissed her before he helped her slide off his lap, mostly naked and tantalizing, into her seat. She dove for her purse.

They both dealt with the calls while they grabbed their clothes and wiggled into them.

He fished an emergency beacon out of his glove compartment and set it on the top of his car. The rotating light washed the grass and tree limbs with red swirls.

"He's hit again," he said as he started the car. "We've got a live victim on the Eisenhower Expressway five minutes away from Chicago Regional."

"I know," she said. "They're trying to patch me in to the paramedics now."

He thrust the gearshift into reverse, tossed his arm over his seat and floored the accelerator. "Seat belt on?"

She nodded.

He backed the car down the path full tilt. Seatbelts strained as the impacts from the bumpy road jolted them in their seats. The tires hit asphalt and he slammed on the brakes. All the anti-skid devices in the car engaged with a mechanical moan and they fishtailed onto the road. He floored the car again and they took off.

He wanted to tell her what their trip to lovers lane meant to him. But there'd be time for that later.

Against Doctor's Orders

by

K.M. Daughters

Against Doctor's Orders

Cover Art by *Kim Mendoza*

The Wild Rose Press
PO Box 708
Adams Basin, NY 14410-0706
Visit us at www.thewildrosepress.com

Publishing History
First Crimson Rose Edition, 2008
Print ISBN 1-60154-350-6

Published in the United States of America

DEDICATION:

For Kay and Mickey

ACKNOWLEDGEMENT:

We wish to thank Dr. Brandon Kramer, Dr. Mike Maugeri and Lieutenant Frank Cargola for providing us with your expertise. A special thanks to Lucy - your reaction made all the difference.

Prologue

Darkness is my friend.

It holds me, warms me and protects me. She thinks she is punishing me. Let her think I am afraid in the closet. She doesn't know anything. But soon, very soon, she will know what punishment truly means. It won't be long now. I am almost ready. Not much longer and I'll get free.

Voices. I put my hands over my ears, but I still hear them. She pleads with him again. What an actress. She pretends that she cares what he does to me. But she doesn't. She lets him come to the closet. Again and again he comes.

Pain is not my friend.

It takes me away from the darkness. I try to get back to the darkness. I try and try. Last time I cried, but this time I won't. No, I won't make a sound. I am a strong boy. I can do this. He hurts my body, but I won't cry out. Not this time.

I stare at the red hair and the clown-painted face. I hate you. I hate you.

She pleads again. Tells him, "Hurry. Put him back in the closet."

He hits me in the face. I taste the blood in my mouth. Almost there. Almost back. See how strong I

1

have grown? Not one sound. Not one cry. I can feel it. It is close. Soon I'll be alive and free.

I am ready. I curl my fingers around the knife. She did not see me grab it from the table. I am invisible to her. I waited until I was strong enough to use it. I am strong enough now. Be ready. Ready to strike. He opens the door. He reaches in. I move further back.

He yells, "Come out of there!"

No. You come to me.

He leans in. The knife tears through his throat. Blood, so much blood. He falls on my legs. He is very heavy. I push him off of me. He will never hurt me again.

The clown face screams and screams. She tries to run. I reach out and grab her long hair. I wrap it around my fingers. I tug hard. See what a strong boy I am, Momma. She falls. I stand over her. She is afraid now. She begs.

Shut up, bitch. Just shut up. The knife enters her chest so smoothly. Again and again. So smoothly. Finally, she is quiet. Her eyes stare at me. I use my new friend, the knife, to make her stop staring at me. Stop looking at me. Stop looking at me.

****

The police captain found the little boy curled near his mother's corpse, his puny body drenched with her blood. Red hair pooled around his knobby knees. He grasped a bloody knife in bony little fingers. The skeletal child never said a word as they wrapped him in a blanket and helped him to the waiting ambulance.

Something in those penetrating eyes raised goose bumps on the cop's arms. When he tried to explain it to his wife that night, he was at a loss for words. All John Sullivan could say was, "Today I looked into the eyes of evil."

Chapter 1

Doctor Molly Jordan's jacket was covered with the officer's blood. She hadn't noticed. Seconds after the drenched, sticky clothes were cut away from his body, she determined the entry site of the bullet. The trauma team moved with expert precision, like one body with twelve hands, taking their cues from Molly's soft steady voice. She didn't permit spare words or actions in her ER.

"Get a type and cross match for him, Trudy," she directed.

"Way ahead of you." Trudy responded. Expectantly, the young Physicians Assistant looked toward the glass partition. "Two bags of O-pos are on their way down from the bank. He's a donor. Came in just yesterday. We can go autologous and give him his own blood for now."

Molly nodded, satisfied, and examined the unconscious man.

"Airway's clear. No other trauma." She looked up at the monitor. "Pulse and pressure are too low. Get that blood hung."

Trudy took two units from the nurse who rushed into the room. In seconds the transfusion started.

"Give me more compression at the site. Good." Molly straightened, stepped back from the glare of the overhead lamp, and ripped her surgical mask down below her chin.

"Get him to the CT scanner. Page Michael Lynch and tell him we've got a Level 1 trauma coming up to OR." She tugged off her gloves with dual snaps of latex and dumped them in a receptacle near the door. "Trudy, keep up compression and ride the cart with him."

Molly watched as the P.A. straddled the man's body and leaned into palm over palm pressure where his neck and right shoulder met. A dark splotch of blood bloomed crimson on the sterile gauze beneath Trudy's hands.

Two other members of the team sprang unbidden and manned the gurney front and back to steer it toward the door.

Molly walked out of the room behind the gurney and turned to speak with two officers who held vigil on the other side of the glass partition. She knew they were cops even though they weren't in uniform.

Well worn, sports jackets rumpled from physical exertion, all but matching ties, black dress slacks belted with distressed leather, and shoulder holster bulges, spelled law enforcement. Both men also wore muddy stripes of their comrade's blood on their clothes.

A pang of memory of her fallen husband pierced her. She offered her hand to each in turn.

"Dr. Molly Jordan." She met the eyes of the older of the two. "Officer?"

"Detectives Barnes and Sullivan, ma'am."

A mitt, double the size of Molly's, clenched her delicate hand. Barnes tilted his head in the younger cop's direction. "Joey here is Danny's brother. Lieutenant Daniel Sullivan. Homicide. How is he? He's going to make it, right?"

4

Molly eased her hand from Barnes' damp grip and looked at Joey. She saw the family resemblance. He had the same general build, an aquiline nose, high cheekbones and a strong jaw line like his brother. Cornflower blue eyes stared at her, worry lines etched on his face.

"He's lost a lot of blood, Detective Sullivan," she said. "We have the bleeding in check and stabilized him enough for surgery. Our Surgical Chief has been notified. He's the best there is. We're transfusing him with blood he donated yesterday and he has a common blood type if he needs more."

"We're the same type." Joey plucked at the button on his shirt cuff. "I can give him blood."

"It isn't necessary. We've got it under control so far." Molly smiled, meant to reassure, and garnered shaky grins from both men. She patted Joe's arm and turned toward Barnes. "You bring him in?"

"Yeah." Barnes ran his hand through wispy, gray-streaked brown hair. "It went down fast. Nobody knew there was a shooter. Danny dove to cover Joey and got picked off in mid-air. Still managed to plug the shooter, though. Our backup came and EMS still hadn't, so Joey and I got Danny in the car and headed here. I drove; Joey rode in back and put pressure on Danny's neck. Jesus. He was bleeding bad. Couldn't wait for EMS. They brought in the shooter. With luck the bastard died."

Joey shifted from foot to foot and stared at Molly's blood-stained jacket, a pained expression on his face. "When will we know if he's going to be all right, Dr. Jordan?"

"I'll keep checking and if you'll go to the surgical family lounge off the main lobby and sign in, Dr. Lynch will speak with you when he's out of surgery."

"Thanks, Doc." Joey held out his hand toward her.

Molly gave it a quick shake. "Good luck,

detectives. He's in very capable hands."

She turned away and walked toward the administrative desk at the center of the emergency room.

She checked on the condition of the "shooter." The team had done everything possible to revive him, but he had been pronounced dead a few minutes earlier. Regardless of who drew first, Molly's job, as one of the attending physicians of the Chicago Regional Trauma Center, held precious every life.

Names paired with injury or illness covered the patient board and Molly suspected the outer waiting area was standing room only. Flu season had begun and a freaky pre-winter snowfall early that morning brought victims of fender-benders off snow-filmed roads and those who'd fallen on slick concrete into the ER for medical attention.

Adrenaline high, Molly changed her jacket and whirled in and out of the circular pattern of rooms, served her team and treated patients, the way she preferred to practice medicine. She needed to keep busy. The injured cop had stirred painful memories. She remembered Eddie lying on a similar table, beneath similar hands, blood draining. Would it have made a difference if they had been her hands? She would always be helpless to do anything but wonder.

Thoughts of Eddie always turned to thoughts of their daughter, Amy. Molly checked her watch. Amy would get home from school soon and Bobbie would cluck over her and keep up with her non-stop conversation while she fixed her a snack. Molly wished daily that she could do these things with her daughter instead of her live-in housekeeper, but with her erratic hours, Bobbie was a godsend.

Molly hoped she could make good on the promise to help Amy on her fifth grade science project that night. Her shift ended in a half hour and her workday should be over. In her experience when it came to adherence to a shift schedule in a chaotic emergency room, what should be rarely was.

"Molly, I need you in exam 4," a nurse called. "Patient says she won't talk to anybody but you."

She recognized the elderly patient in the exam room at once, but couldn't remember her name. She lay propped on pillows on the bed, a starched white sheet stretched taut over her middle. Her cheeks were pinkish and her eyes were clear and alert. She looked content and not particularly sick. Molly gave her a warm smile and opened the metal chart to scan the notations.

The woman smiled wryly in return. "You need a wagon to pull that chart around by now," she quipped.

"How long have you been having chest pain?" Molly set the chart aside and checked the woman's chest with her stethoscope.

"Maybe two days." She took a deep breath and held it at Molly's direction. "My cardiologist told me to come here and get checked instead of seeing him. You took such good care of me when I had that heart attack, I asked for you."

Molly hung the stethoscope around her neck. "We'll do a scan and see what's going on. Your blood work is normal. Are you in much pain now?"

"Not really. I feel pretty good now. It's been hard taking care of my husband. If the cancer doesn't kill him, I will." She belly laughed.

"Take this chance to rest." Molly patted her hand. "I'll check back with you later when we have the results of the scan."

Two hours later, Molly walked out into the ambulance bay and took a deep breath, grateful for the fresh, unseasonably wintry air. Every hospital in the country, and Molly suspected anywhere in the world, had the same smell. Pungent antiseptic odors laced with cleaning fluid fumes were overlaid with the singular, synthetic smell of hospital food. Food shouldn't smell that way.

The wash of fresh air as she left work every day after ten to twelve hours of hospital-smell cleansed her.

She walked to the crosswalk that led to the multi-level, parking structure, hesitated and turned around. She was late anyway and it would only take a few minutes to check on the detective's status. Amy, thank God, was flexible and would forgive the delay.

She checked the grease board in the surgical recovery suite for "Daniel S.", found his name and felt a sudden burst of triumph because he made it through surgery without complications.

She headed toward one of six curtained areas, pushed aside the material that skirted his wheeled bed and picked up his chart. She waited while a nurse repeated his name in a sharp questioning voice to bring him out of his anesthetic sleep.

"DANIEL? DANIEL." His eyeballs rolled beneath closed lids. "That's it, Dan, time to open your eyes."

"Yuuh…" he garbled.

The nurse worked with efficient grace, checked drainage tubes and talked to him in a conversational tone. "Would you like to go to your room soon, Dan?"

He nodded and uttered a guttural sound.

"Okay. Just a little while longer and we'll get you out of here." The nurse took the chart from Molly and wrote some quick entries. She handed the chart back. "He's all yours, Dr. Jordan."

Alone with the half-asleep man, Molly stole a moment to appreciate the muscled torso and long, black eyelashes that softened the hard planes of his face. He looked innocent and vulnerable.

She imagined that the eyes beneath his closed lids were glacier blue, direct as an x-ray and anything but innocent when they were open.

She shivered. How long had it been since she thought like a woman? A shimmer of attraction to a fine figure of a male coursed through her. His hands rested at his sides and even in repose she could appreciate their capability for power. What would it feel like to be caressed by those strong hands? What would it feel like to be cared for instead of always taking care of others?

His eyes fluttered open. She was wrong and she was right about those slumbering eyes. Wrong, because they weren't polar blue, but Emerald Isle green. Right, because they were direct as an x-ray as they bored into her eyes.

"Where…?" He flicked his tongue around dry lips.

Molly reached for a cup of ice chips at his bedside, brought one to his lips and wet them in a slow circle. "Is that better, Dan?"

His breath was warm against her wrist. The sensation and the magnetic force of his eyes made her shiver again.

She methodically dried her hand with a tissue and regained her practiced, professional composure. "I'm Doctor Jordan. I treated you in the ER. You've just had surgery to remove the bullet."

His eyelids dipped and a frown line furrowed his brow as he struggled to keep his eyes open. "Shot." His sleepy green eyes stared at her again.

She nodded.

"Joey?" He grasped her forearm and held on to it.

The physical contact made her weak-kneed and confused that she should feel such heat and power from a man in Sullivan's state. It wasn't reasonable that she should feel any physical attraction to a patient.

She avoided his eyes and removed his hand from her arm on the pretense of taking his pulse. She hoped he wouldn't notice that a monitor on the wall behind him already displayed his pulse rate and other vital signs.

"Your brother Joe is fine. I talked with him and another officer after you left my ER." Her voice sounded muffled, squeaky with tension and foreign to her ears.

"Good," he said. His head nodded. "Tired."

"You should rest." Molly placed his arm gently at his side. She leaned over him to check the bandage on his neck. "Are you right-handed, Dan?"

"Mm hm."

"Your right arm is going to be stiff," she advised him.

Her head spun as his left arm circled her back and tilted her closer to him. Her breath caught when her abdomen pressed against the side of his bed and heightened the potent sexual surge that plummeted inside her.

"This arm works fine," he teased.

She tried to stand straight when a throat-clear rasped behind her, but he wouldn't let her go.

"I need to examine him, doctor," the nurse said.

"Of course." Molly swiveled carefully to break Dan's grip without jarring him and stepped back, still shaky from the never-before sensual reaction to a patient.

He aimed a blissful half-grin at both women, blinked once and slept.

****

The time it took to commute home from the hospital usually allowed her to shift from her role as Doctor Jordan to Amy's Mommy, and just plain Molly. She always avoided expressway driving and chose local routes to forestall traffic tie-ups. At that time of day, just shy of dinner hour, any East/West road toward or away from Chicago jammed up and she couldn't avoid traffic congestion no matter which route she took.

While her car chugged along and idled, she passed time looking at the trees and patches of lawn that lined Roosevelt Road, the morning slush long since melted. She tried to deep breathe herself into a peaceful state and appreciate the greenery that wouldn't be around much longer. In another month, everything would be gray twigs and hay-colored grass.

Even with the interruptions of red lights and slow progress home, most days Molly could enjoy the car ride and let the events of her workday slip away. But concern for Dan Sullivan lingered, along with the faint elevator-fall sensation she felt with his arm wrapped around her.

She flipped open her phone, called the main ER desk and asked for Trudy. She hung up and waited for her P.A. to respond to her page. Near home Molly's phone rang.

"Hey, Trudy. I'm checking on a patient. Sullivan. Daniel Sullivan. The cop with the bullet wound. Is he out of recovery?"

"Hold on. I'll check."

Molly pulled into her driveway, careful not to tag the bike on the grass near the concrete apron. She triggered the electronic opener but sat in the car outside the garage, phone propped to her ear.

"Yes, he's out. He's listed in stable but guarded condition." Trudy laughed, a contagious riff that made Molly laugh, too.

"What?"

"I'd say Daniel Sullivan is in excellent condition. Yummmm."

"Trudy. Where's your professional decorum?" Molly eased the car forward, smiling. "Page me if there's any negative change in his condition, okay? Otherwise, I'll see you tomorrow. Have a good evening. Are you off soon?"

"Should have been gone about an hour ago, but I'll get there. Say hello to Bobbie for me and give that little one a squeeze."

"I will," Molly promised.

She snapped her phone shut, pulled her silver, beetle convertible into the three-car garage, next to the older weathered blue Jeep, and went into her house. She shut the door behind her, leaned her head against it, closed her eyes and let her home fill her senses.

Voices murmured over the muted sounds of the TV. Something wonderful cooking in the kitchen made her stomach growl. She hadn't eaten anything since the power protein bar Bobbie tossed to her as she left for the hospital that morning.

She always used the twenty-mile commute back to the western suburbs to clear her mind so that the ER never infringed on her home life with Amy. The drive that day did nothing to clear away thoughts of Dan Sullivan. Concern for a patient frequently stayed with her and governed her off-hours actions, but there was no genuine medical reason for her preoccupation with Dan.

She shook her head. *What is wrong with me? Why would I want another cop?*

Chapter 2

The comfort of her haven enveloped Molly as she turned the TV off in the empty family room and then walked through the rear hallway of her immaculate home toward the front foyer. A gilded, antique chandelier cast muted light down from twenty feet over her head and made the satin finish of the natural cherry wood floors glow pinkish red.

She leaned against one of the carved balusters on the bottom of the central staircase and eased out of her shoes, using her toes to push them off at the back of her heels.

"Hello," she called up the stairs.

"Hi Doc. I'll be right down," came Bobbie's greeting. "There's a new wine breathing on the counter that I want you to try with that cheese you like. Help yourself and let me know what you think."

Bobbie's current culinary phase made every dinner an adventure. Most evenings the unusual recipes were delicious. That night's experiment smelled tempting.

Roberta Leighton was more like a younger sister to Molly than an employee. She had hired Bobbie when her maternity leave after Amy was

13

born. Then a teenager taking a smattering of college courses that ran the gamut of the arts and sciences, Bobbie had always been flaky when it came to her big-picture career direction. However, her loyalty, dependability and devotion to Amy and Molly had never wavered.

"Hi, Momma." Amy hung over the banister with a portable phone pressed to her ear and her long, sable hair semi-contained in a scrunchie. "I'm on the phone with Mary. I'll be right down."

Molly shook her head at her daughter. Not yet ten and she already had a telephone-gabbing addiction. "Okay, honey, but make it fast. I missed you and I need a hug, real bad." Molly bent over and massaged her aching toes.

"Did you put Humpty back together?" Amy sang out the customary question.

"Yes, I put Humpty back together." Her heart swelled with love for her little girl as she walked into the kitchen to wait for her welcome hug.

She poured a glass of wine and took a deep, satisfying sip. *Bobbie is a marvel.*

Molly stared out the bay window beyond her oval-shaped dining table at the wooded yard dotted with wheat colored prairie grass, fat evergreens, and wildflower stems. When she built the house she wanted a peaceful refuge, a yard where Amy could play and gardens where Molly could dig in the dirt to her heart's content.

During inclement weather when she couldn't be outside, she loved gazing out her windows at the lovely vista. That evening she didn't see the evergreen trees that lined her property or the perennial beds and shrubs she lovingly tended in the Spring and Summer, even though solar energy lights illuminated the perimeter of her land. She saw instead the mammoth, stone library in New York, where she and Eddie had taken Amy for a children's story hour, seven years ago.

They had planned to drop their daughter off for the well-supervised session and grab a cup of coffee together, while Amy enjoyed the company of other three year olds. But neither of them could bear to leave Amy alone. They hid behind the bookshelves to watch their little girl and giggled at their own silliness like the children gathered in a sloppy circle around the reader.

When the librarian finished reading the *Humpty Dumpty* nursery rhyme, Amy raised her tiny hand to speak.

"*My* mommy put Humpty back together," she asserted with absolute conviction.

Her daughter's innocent, unconditional confidence in her abilities as a healer had melted her heart. It still did. From that day on, whenever she came home from work, Eddie and Amy asked if she put Humpty together again. After Eddie's death, Amy asked the question alone. Her daughter remained confident in her even though she couldn't put her daddy back together.

Eddie. Molly still ached for him and yearned for the easy intimacy they had shared. Watching their little girl grow was so hard without him. They had wonderful dreams and plans for Amy and for themselves. They wanted more children, a bigger house and a family vacation when Molly finished her residency. Eddie was taken away from them too soon.

He had been on the front-line when the World Trade Center fell on September 11th and had survived the perils of that terrible day. They couldn't believe the gift. Panic sweat had dripped off her while she worked triage in the New York ER turned M.A.S.H. unit all day, until at last she had word that Eddie was alive. The blessing was short-lived. A month later in a random, senseless instant, he was killed at a local liquor store hold-up.

Bobbie bounded into the kitchen fiddling with loose ends of her waist-length, strawberry hair, come undone from the knot at the top of her head.

"How was your day? You look beat, Doc. What do you think of the wine?" She rattled off questions as she headed for the stove.

With Roberta around, Molly had little chance to linger in the past.

"It's delicious. What is it?"

"It's a *Catena Malbec*. Can you taste the black cherry and the touch of black pepper?"

"No." Molly took another healthy swig and swished it around her mouth.

"Neither can I and who cares?" Bobbie laughed as she lifted the cover off a pot and set a puff of steam free. She picked up a giant ladle from a ceramic spoon-rest on the counter and stirred the bubbling soup.

"Laura Catena spoke about her winery in Argentina during my class last night and we had a small wine tasting. I really enjoyed the Malbec and thought you would, too."

"You know my tastes so well. This is perfect. How's the class going?"

"Oh, fine. Much better than last semester. At least I found out last semester that I really don't want to be an auto mechanic. But, hey, look at all the money I save us by doing our oil changes now. I think I'm going to take a belly dancing class next semester."

Molly breathed in the spicy aroma in the kitchen. "How about culinary school? Your cooking is amazing."

"There's so much out there to experience. Never did figure out what to do with my degree. I just can't seem to find one thing and stick with it. I'm always tempted to try something new. Did you always want to be a doctor?"

Molly pulled out a chair and relaxed at the table. "I knew since I was five years old. I never changed my mind or considered anything else."

"How could you know something that important when you were so young?" Bobbie walked away from the stove and leaned over the granite-topped peninsula that separated her from Molly.

"We had this great pediatrician when I was a little girl," Molly related. "I hated getting my shots before I started kindergarten. I think it's my first clear memory of childhood. I told Dr. Cole that one day I would be a doctor and give *him* shots. He and my mother thought it was funny. But I wasn't kidding."

"A career born of revenge." Bobbie laughed.

"He walked into the hospital where I worked about four years ago. He was there to go on an insulin pump to control his diabetes and he asked me if I would like to give him one of his last insulin shots."

"You didn't. Did you?"

"You bet I did, and it was the best shot I ever gave—a real full circle moment."

"Maybe someday soon I'll find something that I want as much as you did."

Amy ran into the kitchen on a bead for her mother. Her silky, dark hair flew away from her freckled face and her green eyes sparkled. Molly stood up and Amy launched her lithe, little body into her open arms. She hugged her mother tight.

"I missed you, Mom. I missed you so much." She squeezed her eyes shut in apparent ecstasy.

Molly gave Bobbie a questioning look over the top of Amy's head. Bobbie shrugged her shoulders.

"Amy, my love. Why do I have the feeling I'm being buttered up for something?"

"I did miss you. Honestly I did. I love you so

much." She squeezed into the hug again.

"And I love you. Now spill it, please. What do you want?" Molly held her daughter gently at arms' length and searched her face.

"Well…" Amy said, her expression earnest. "Now that Mary and I are turning ten we can be junior Charity Girls, and Mary asked her mom, and her mom said, yes and her mom is going to be our…um…her squad leader, and Mary wants to know if I can join, too. We get to help poor kids and sell cookies and earn trips and everything. Can I please, Mom? I want to be a Charity Girl, too. Mary's mom said she would call you tomorrow. Mary's uncle got sick and her mom had to go see him. Please, Momma? Pretty please?"

"I'll talk to Mrs. Lynch tomorrow. If Mary is going to join, I don't see why not, especially since Mrs. Lynch will be your leader."

She threw her arms around Molly in a spontaneous hug. "Thank you *so* much. You are the best mom ever. I've gotta call Mary."

Molly watched her scamper off. "That last hug felt like you meant it, at least," she called after her. "Make it quick. Dinner's ready."

"I'll make it really fast. We get to go on hayrides and dances and even family camping." She pounded up the stairs.

"Camping? Did she just say family camping? Yikes, Bobbie, what did I just get us into?"

"Whoa. What's this, 'us', business? I tried camping once. Once was more than enough. Like auto repair, I learned. I don't do camping."

"Thanks, pal. I thought I could count on you."

"You can. Just not in a tent with bugs."

"People camp everyday. How hard can it be?"

Molly took a spoon out of a drawer and lifted the lid off the pot on the stove. "It's so good to see Amy excited about something."

She dipped the spoon and sampled the fragrant broth. "Mmm, the soup is delicious. What is it?"

"Escarole with beans and Italian sausage."

"I'm really going to hate to see the semester end. This culinary class is a winner."

"Next semester I'll just have to teach you to belly dance."

"Camping, belly dancing, what next?"

"Don't tell Amy you heard it from me, but roller-skating is next. Amy has her heart set on a birthday party next week at the skating rink."

"Good Lord, more wine."

Molly enjoyed dinnertime when nothing else mattered but the comfort of good food and the music of her little girl's voice. She loved the togetherness, the ability to reach out and touch a strand of Amy's shiny hair or brush her arm with her hand. Amy entertained them with stories of her day at school. She could sit and listen to her daughter for hours.

Molly waited to speak until Amy wound down and focused on eating her soup. "Honey, I was thinking. I have Saturday off. Why don't you ask Mary if she wants to sleep over on Friday night? I'll stop and get pizza on the way home and we can have a girls' night. Then Saturday morning we could all go to the skating rink and see if it's not too late to schedule a birthday party for next weekend. What do you think?"

Amy's face froze. "Do you mean it? Can I really have a skating party? Mom, you are the best! How did you know that's what I wanted?"

"Mother's know everything. For instance, I know before you rush off to call Mary again, you're going to clear the table and load the dishwasher."

That evening, after the latest Harry Potter book was closed on Amy's bedside table, Molly walked around her living room and switched lights off. They had completed the dreaded science project, followed by Amy's long bubble bath. Her hair pinned up in a bun, her little body shiny with soapy water, Molly loved watching her daughter when unaware she was being observed.

Molly lingered in the darkened, hushed room surrounded by the things she prized. An inviting place to sit, she regretted she didn't use that room more.

They seemed to congregate in the back of the house where the huge kitchen connected to a cozy family room with Mission style furnishings and a cushiony black leather couch. She never thought to light the fire in the stone hearth there or in the living room. The evenings flew by with no time to unwind before a fire. *Life shouldn't be so rushed. But between work and a ten year old, it just is.*

She enjoyed the tranquil feeling of having the house to herself a while longer before she walked around the rest of the ground floor. She twisted dead bolt mechanisms on front and back doors and double-checked the lock on the patio sliding doors. Eddie had been adamant about such things and the habit was ingrained in her.

She entered her bedroom suite off the front foyer through elegant carved French doors and tapped in the code to arm the security system on a wall keypad. She had the builder change the library in the original design into a first-floor bedroom and bath for her, so that any middle-of-the-night phone calls wouldn't disturb her household.

The hardest decision Molly ever made was to leave the home she and Eddie had made together. In New York the memories were ever-present on every street they traveled and in every corner of their home. She was glad that she no longer had to pass by the liquor store where Eddie was shot. The Attending Physician spot in Chicago seemed like a good opportunity for Molly to advance her career and start fresh after living with daily reminders of the sudden loss of her husband.

She loved her new work and took pride in the trauma center's expanding services and stellar reputation. But witnessing Amy's tentative flowering here was what she loved most about their new life and gave her much-needed affirmation that she'd made the right choices for them.

She hurried her shower, even though the hot pulsing spray did wonders for her myriad of dull aches. She slipped into the homey warmth of her favorite flannel pajamas and climbed into her king-sized bed. Clean and comfortable, she snuggled under the down comforter, adjusted the pillows behind her and selected the new romantic suspense novel she'd been relishing off the top of a stack of medical journals on her bedside table. After devouring only a few pages her eyes grew heavy.

Her hands caressed the rippled muscular chest, brushing over silky hair. She thrilled at the contrast of her soft skin against taut male flesh. His rough hands pulled the front of her pajamas open and sent a spray of buttons clacking on the floor on either side of the bed. He pushed the cloth off her shoulders. Her nipples swelled and hardened as the cool air brushed against her naked skin. Fire charged through her awakening body as he closed his moist mouth over one breast. He clasped her body closer as he feasted on that breast, then the other. Her stomach clenched as his head moved unhurried, down, covering every inch of her torso. She moved beneath his lips in involuntary waves. She felt the stubble of his beard scrape against her ribs. His teeth clasped the waistband of her pajama pants and inched them down. Her legs parted as if she had no choice. Her mind was capable of only one thought. More. Dan, give me more. She moaned.

She jolted half out of bed. The covers heaved and

the motion flung the book on the floor. Disoriented, her eyes darted until she recognized the familiar room. A warm flush surged over her body and her pulse raced. *What was that all about?*

She hadn't given sex a thought for a long time. Why did the sight of one lean, muscular body have her panting in her sleep? How many naked males had she seen during her voluntary celibacy? Not one of them had stirred any reaction in her, other than clinical. What was it about this man that unleashed the passion she had buried deep inside since Eddie's death?

She grabbed a medical journal off the end table and paged to an article about adamantine resistance among influenza-A viruses—guaranteed to induce coma-like sleep in minutes. She read the first paragraph and her mind drifted back to the dream. Her bed felt cold and empty. What would it be like to have a man in her life again? She wanted that. But she wanted a man who would stay with her. Just like Eddie, Dan was a cop. She was convinced a man like him would never stay.

Chapter 3

Officers of the law from three surrounding communities flagrantly broke the rules. Only two visitors at a time were allowed in the intensive care unit of Chicago Regional Hospital and the cops knew it. They pretended they didn't.

The diligent receptionist gave up trying to rein the men in. Most of them didn't stop at her desk to register anyway—another one of the rules they ignored. They pushed through the glass doors into the visitor waiting area and strode past the smiling receptionist who strained forward, pen in hand. They touched the corners of their hats, winked or gave her a lazy wave as they rounded the corner to the elevator banks on their way to visit Daniel Sullivan.

At times, there were clusters of eight or nine men in front of Dan's ten by ten hi-tech, intensive care suite, as they used up their off-duty hours to visit one of their own. Danny was the center of their attention around the clock after his surgery.

When he slept, the men stood guard and whispered pleasantries to the medical personnel who nudged past them to check on their patient. When

Danny awoke, groggy and fuzzyheaded, the men pushed forward into the cramped space, glad to hear whatever small utterances Danny managed.

Mrs. Sullivan wouldn't leave her son's bedside that first night, so they brought her coffees, sodas, donuts, and fast food, which she politely refused with tired smiles. Courteous, silent and vigilant, they believed in the power of the bond between them. They were there for Danny and it would pull him through.

They kept the off-color remarks to a minimum in deference to Danny's mother. Their remarks to Danny were light as if his situation were no big deal.

"Just a scratch, Danny boy."

"Don't get too used to R&R."

"You don't expect us to be nice to you, do you?"

"Twenty-four hours, and then we'll kick your ass out of that bed...excuse me, Mrs. Sullivan."

****

Twenty-four hours after surgery, Danny was wide-awake and itchy to get out. Pinioned to the bed by IV lines and machine cables, he felt like a lab specimen. He assured his mother that she could go home for a shower and a nap. He enjoyed the banter with his buddies and fellow officers. Word traveled among the members of the police force and whether they knew Danny personally or not, they came to see him in a show of solidarity and respect.

He savored the slow progress he made toward freedom with each tube or catheter removal. And he hounded nurses, technicians and doctors to let him go home.

"What's this?" A petite woman in a starched, sky blue lab jacket shouldered her way through the line of men in front of Danny's suite.

She reached the foot of his bed, turned her back to him and faced off with his visitors. "I need to examine my patient. Please go downstairs to the visitor's lounge and I'll notify the receptionist when you can return. No more than two at a time."

He leaned forward to check out her rear end while she pulled sliding, glass-pocket doors from the sidewalls and closed them in the suite together. Beyond the doors the men ambled away, obedient for the moment.

She pivoted around and her pretty blue eyes stared at him.

He smiled and leaned back into the pillow. "Well, hello."

"Hello," she said, looking too serious, yet vulnerable.

Her head bent to read his chart. *Maureen Jordan, M.D.* per the tag pinned on her coat. Short platinum blonde hair shone white in the halo of florescent light and spiked around her creamy complexion on a heart shaped face. Her features were delicate. The hands that held his medical chart had long tapered fingers, short unpolished nails and no wedding ring.

She gave him a discerning once over with a keen clinical gaze. "You're looking a lot better than you did last night. How are you feeling?"

"Like shit." He forced a half smile up at her.

She put the metal clipboard aside. "How's the pain?"

"I'm still leaning towards the frown side of your little frown/smile pain graph," he said, pointing to the illustration on the wall.

She moved closer to his bed and fiddled with the electronic device that dispensed pain medication. "Are you pushing the button for medication as you need it?"

"Liberally." He grinned. "Morphine's a beautiful thing. Truth serum. I must have told my mother I loved her ten times."

She laughed. "I'm going to listen to your heart."

She pulled a stethoscope from her jacket pocket and tugged the string to loosen his hospital gown. She warmed the chest piece with her hands and leaned over him.

"Lilacs," he said. "I remember smelling lilacs last night."

"Oh, my perfume?" She straightened. "I was in the recovery room when you were brought out of anesthesia. It was more like late yesterday afternoon than last night. I'm sure your sense of time is a little confused."

She stood, hands in her coat pocket, her huge eyes full of concern. He thought about the curves under her lab coat and felt a lot better for the fantasy.

"Then it's you I should thank, Doctor Maureen Jordan...for saving my life."

"Uh...no. It's Molly...Doctor Molly Jordan. Nobody calls me Maureen, except my mother." She pulled on the ends of her hair with one hand. "And you're welcome. But your surgeon had more to do with saving your life than I did. I'm an attending in the ER."

"Don't be modest. Thank you, Molly." He caught hold of her hand as she moved it away from her face and brought her palm to his lips.

A sizzle of pleasure seemed mutual, even as her arm stiffened and pulled against him. He cupped her hand and placed it over his heart. The soft expression on her face changed to something like alarm as he released her hand.

"My patients call me Dr. Jordan," she said, prudish and formal. "Is there anything you need to make you more comfortable?"

"Climb into bed with me, Molly, and we'll see." He patted the covers next to him.

"What a flirt." She backed a foot away from his bed. "I think I'll leave you to the ICU nurses now."

26

She turned to go.

"Whoa, not so fast," he said. "When do I get out of here?"

She turned back and picked up his chart again. "Have you been up yet?"

"Yeah, last night. Stood up and sat back down. They say I graduate to sitting in the chair soon."

"I'll leave orders to move you to a room on one of the general floors by tonight if you continue to improve."

"General floors?" He balked at the thought. "Send me home today. I'll recuperate better there."

"I'll decide when you go home." She bristled. "What kind of a support system do you have for caretaking? Is there a Mrs. Sullivan?"

"Why yes, there is." Was that disappointment he saw flash through her baby blues? "You just missed her, as a matter of fact."

"Good." She cradled his chart in the crook of her arm. "In a day or two we'll go over discharge instructions with you both if your condition warrants release. Let the nurses know if you need anything."

She pulled the sliding doors open, marched over to the nurses' desk and wrote in his chart, her back to him.

"Molly," he called.

"Yes, Mr. Sullivan," she answered, her back still toward him.

She didn't lift her head from her work, but he was sure that her fair skin blushed a hot pink with his familiarity in front of her peers.

"Stick around and meet Mrs. Sullivan. I like to introduce my mother to my sweethearts."

She hurried away without a word, her cheeks scarlet.

Chapter 4

Stop looking. Stop looking at me. Leave me alone. Why can't you just stay dead? You think I don't see you watching everything I put in my cart. You have no say anymore, Ma. I can eat whatever I want. I can do whatever I want. I don't have to listen to you. I am free. One more time, Ma. I am warning you. If you look at me one more time, you will be sorry. Don't make me do it.

It's your fault. You made me follow you. Now I am watching you. You didn't see my car pull out behind you. You think you can just ignore me? You think I will just go away? I am the one with the power now, Ma. Don't look so surprised to see me. Don't pretend you don't know me. I warned you to stop looking at me back at the store, but you never listen to me. You never listen.

The crimson hair feels silky in my strong grip. I pull harder and harder until it comes off in my hand. Shut up. Stop screaming. Just shut up, bitch. My knife slips so easily across your throat. Now, into your chest. In and out, in and out. So smooth. I am so strong. I told you to stop. Stop looking at me. My friend, the knife, once again makes you stop looking at me.

****

The young cop, face inflamed with humiliation, could not stop throwing up his lunch. He had answered the call and was the first to look into the open trunk of the car. What he discovered there would probably cause him to have nightmares for months.

Joe Sullivan put his hand on the cop's back to assure him he had nothing to be embarrassed about. Truth was, his lunch wasn't setting easy, either.

He gulped back nausea and tried not to feel out of his depth. He focused on the mechanics of working the scene like a homicide investigation textbook, as Danny would have it, were he there instead of lying in a hospital bed. He wished that he were at the hospital instead. Anywhere but here. No one could look at such brutality, such hatred, and not be changed forever.

****

Molly balanced a cardboard bakery box and a large sack of goodie bags in her arms as she entered the roller rink with Bobbie and Amy.

"I thought I was so clever coming an hour early, but this place is bedlam already," she lamented.

She hadn't beaten the weekend crowd to set up for Amy's birthday party as she had hoped. The swarm of skaters who looped around ahead of her made her dizzy. A force field of excitement pulsed off Amy, skipping along at her side. They followed the be-skated teenager, who identified herself as their party hostess at the door, through a labyrinth of assorted tables and chairs.

"These are your tables." The hostess pointed with bored detachment, like the minor arm movement required major exertion, to two rectangular tables draped in red plastic. The girl managed to slouch, even on roller-skates. The

29

maroon ends of her black hair stuck up in glossy points around her pale face. The added height from her skates put her eye to eye with Molly, and her dark lipstick and rolling gum-chewing riveted Molly's attention to the lazy movements of her slack mouth.

A foreshadowing of what might lie in wait for her with Amy shuddered through her. *Give me strength.*

"Okay. Thanks." Molly deposited the cake box on one table and dumped the bulging sack on a chair. "Do I order the pizza now?"

"Yeah. What kind of toppings do you want? You get four large pies with one topping each. Extra toppings cost more. And you get bottomless pitchers of pop with the birthday package." She yawned in Molly's face.

Molly consulted with Amy and Bobbie, and they placed the order.

The hostess dug in the deep pocket of an apron tied around her waist and brought out a handful of tickets. "How many skate rental tickets do you need? Twelve are included in the package."

She asked for ten tickets and watched the hostess skate away with nonchalant grace. She marveled that someone who seemed to lack any energy could push the skates at all.

As they organized their tables, one for the girls, the other for their moms, Amy gabbed away and watched the door for arrivals with eager anticipation.

Dusty beams of sunlight angled down from dirt-streaked windows, high above floor level in the barn-like building. Skates scuffed the ancient floorboards and kept time with the pounding bass of the soft-rock music that blared from speakers rimming the rink. A deejay boomed at intervals: forward skate, backward, couples only, kids only, and adults only.

The music beat inside Molly. Her hips swayed involuntarily as she stood and watched the constant swirl of movement. Her eyes misted when teenage couples looped in front of her, hands clasped tight, their bodies leaned into each other suggestively. Soon, some other mother of a little one might watch Amy and an unreliable looking boy do this couples-skate-dance in their own private oblivion. Molly sighed dreading that day.

Over the next hour little girls toting gift bags and wrapped boxes led their mothers toward Amy, who now wore an identifying cardboard tiara. The girls smiled shy hellos to Mrs. Jordan, returned Amy's delighted squeals and fell in sync with her jabbering. They abandoned the grown-ups the instant Molly handed them a skate rental ticket.

Molly was an eager hostess. She hadn't taken the time for new friendships since she moved to Chicago. She hoped today would be an opportunity to change that. After the group exchanged pleasantries and herded on line to pick up their rental skates, they did what mothers invariably do when they are out with their kids. They forgot about themselves and watched their children have fun. The girls skated on coltish legs, arms linked, four-wide around the rink.

"I think I'm going deaf from the music."

"Whaaaaat? Sorry that was lame."

"It's better than Chuck E. Cheese's," Molly said. The ladies turned toward her and nodded their agreement. "Up until this year, that's the only party place Amy wanted. Afterwards, it took hours for my ears to stop ringing."

Molly watched the girls pass near them again. "We're missing Mary and Kay. She's been having such a difficult pregnancy. I hope she's not battling morning sickness again."

"She's hanging over a bowl cursing Mike's

31

manhood right about now," a man quipped behind her.

Molly turned toward the resonant bass voice and looked up into an alluring male's face, dimpled with a wide smile and topped with mesmerizing tropical sea eyes. Dan Sullivan. Mary Lynch clung to his hand until she spotted Amy and the girls. She shot out onto the rink with her shoes on and ran into a group hug.

"Dan?" Molly barely recognized him. Hard to believe he was the same man that bled all over her in the emergency room a little over a week ago.

He acknowledged Molly with a smile and directed an introduction to her guests. "I'm Mary's uncle Danny." He gave polite handshakes to the women around the table and ended with Molly. His gentle hold on her hand had a far from gentle effect on her.

A feverish burst whipped through her and she feared that her cheeks blushed crimson. A quick incendiary flash in his eyes told Molly he noticed her reaction and took cocky pleasure in it. The exchange took seconds but Molly felt suspended, frozen in the powerful attraction.

She kept her expression passive, pleasant, and let go of his hand. "I had no idea you were related to Mary, Danny. And to Mike and Kay, as well."

She took the wrapped package he held out to her and put it with other presents stacked on Amy's chair.

"Kay's my little sister." He took a seat at the Moms' table and smiled at Molly, apparently comfortable surrounded by ladies.

"Are you staying, Danny?"

"I plan to." He looked around the table. "Unless this is a girls only event?"

Molly's guests talked over each other, "No, no."

"Stay."

32

"Yes, stay."

She poured some soda into his glass. "You're looking well. How are you feeling?"

"Good as new. I'm bored stiff in the house." He dripped charm around the table at the ladies. "I feel fine."

"Well, good." Molly's face burned. "There's a skate rental ticket for Mary there on the table."

"Thanks." He looked deep into her eyes, a half smile on his face, and stood.

She didn't break the stare, which forced her head to angle back a long way with his ascent at least a foot above her.

"I'll go get Mary," he said in a low voice. He walked toward the rink.

The mothers weren't watching their children anymore.

"Nice buns."

"Did you see those long eye lashes?"

"Sorry. I haven't looked above his waist since he walked in. The man sure knows how to wear a pair of jeans."

The women hooted.

"You're married, remember?"

"Not dead, just faithful. This really is a great party so far, Molly."

"Hey, Molly. You're not married. We'll live vicariously through you."

Molly smiled and enjoyed the irreverence, secretly thrilled with the coincidence that Danny was related to Amy's best friend.

She had been off work the two consecutive days after Danny's release from intensive care. By the time she returned to the hospital, he had already been discharged. She didn't realize until now that not seeing him again made her feel a little blue.

He sure cleaned up well. He was good looking at his worst in the hospital with his black beard stubble and matted hair. But clean-shaven with fresh-washed, glossy raven hair, wearing a chest-hugging, dove-colored, cashmere sweater and snug black jeans, his looks stole her breath.

He whistled at the edge of the rink, a casual twist of his lips that produced a piercing bell tone. Mary, alerted by the sound, darted over to her uncle, grinning. They walked together to the rental counter.

Molly poured a soda for herself and sat down with her guests. Ten minutes later she spotted Danny and Mary seated on a bench rink side, both lacing up skates.

"Excuse me," she mumbled to the ladies at the table. Lively gleams of busy-bodied interest in the women's eyes followed her when she got to her feet. Her beeline for Danny would probably rivet the group even more as they sipped their soft drinks on the sidelines.

She made it to the bench when he finished tying his skates and pushed upright. He towered over her. Unintimidated, she touched her index finger to his chest. She took a fixed stance in front of him, like an offensive lineman determined to block any forward movement. Irish meadow-green eyes bore into her eyes. Clearly, he didn't appreciate the affront.

"Where do you think you're going, Daniel Sullivan?" she demanded.

"Skating with my niece." He curved a hand on each side of her waist and steered her out of his path.

She repositioned in front of him and held her ground. "No, you're not. You shouldn't be skating. Good Lord, I'll bet you even drove here, didn't you?"

He didn't respond and she had her answer.

"Did you even read your discharge orders before you left the hospital?" she asked with a take-no-prisoners inflection.

He crossed his arms in front of his chest. She felt a surge of guilty pleasure at the flex of biceps involved, but stood firm.

"No. Did those orders say something about driving?" He steered her out of his way again. "There's no reason I can't drive a car. And a little skating won't hurt me."

He sprung past her and moved into the swirling flow of skaters on the rink, building speed with each powerful lunge of his legs. He flashed her a defiant smile when he made his first loop.

She felt like an idiot standing there. Patients did whatever the hell they wanted when they left her care and it really frosted her. But he was in front of her and she'd be damned if she would let him hurt himself.

By the time she laced up skates and caught up to him, he had linked hands with the girls, lead man on a v-shaped chain, and hauled them faster and faster behind him. She knew better than to be the last man on either end of that chain, but she grabbed for a hand anyway. A wicked gleam flashed in his eye before he added just enough muscle to loosen her grip and whip her towards the sideboards with the momentum.

She handled it like a roller derby queen. The girls cheered her on, delighted.

Back in the game at the next curve, she intended to retaliate. "Your turn to be at the end of the chain, officer."

She moved into the pack, took Amy's outstretched hand and gained speed to inch into lead position.

Danny stopped short, laughing hard, and caused a chain reaction of arm-tugs. His face blanched as he dropped the little girl's hand on either side of him. He reeled unsteady, eyes closed, the tan leached from his cheeks.

35

By instinct, Molly skated to his side and circled his body with her arm to protect him from the other skaters. She spoke in a low voice, "Hold on to me, Danny. Slow. That's right. Let's get you off this rink."She guided him to a seat on the bench and pressed her hand down on the nape of his neck to lower his head towards his knees. "Breathe slowly. Good. Better?"

His color's improving. Molly kept steady downward pressure on his neck until he gathered enough strength to raise his head.

"Yeah, thanks." He stood, but sat back down when he tottered on his skates.

Molly stood up and reached for his wrist.

He didn't try to dislodge her fingers. His world imbalanced, he was docile. "You smell nice," he said, as his chest expanded with the deep breath she counseled him to take.

Then his male pride must have kicked in. "Don't hover." He pushed up from the bench so that he looked down at the top of her head, still bent over her watch.

By slow degrees she arched her neck upward to focus deep into his eyes with all the authority her years of medical training had vested in her. "I'm not hovering. I'm making sure you don't relapse. Untie those skates."

"Lady, the last short, blue-eyed blonde I took orders from was my mother."

"Shows it's actually possible, doesn't it? Untie those skates, *please*. Then come on over for some pizza." She skated away from him before he could argue.

****

The girls skidded off the rink in front of Dan, bumping into each other, a mess of skinny, tangled arms and tight-lipped concern.

"You okay, Uncle Danny?" Mary hung over him,

another little mother, brows pinched with worry.

"Fine, pipsqueak." He tousled her hair. "I think it's time to eat."

Molly padded around the tables in her socks, a busy hostess, by the time Danny ushered the girls to their table. A soft, sweet look on her face, she catered to her guests; very different from the drill sergeant face she'd worn earlier when she tried to prevent him from skating. He took a seat, cowed that he didn't listen to her advice.

Surrounded by maternal concern over the dizzy spell, he managed to deflect their attention politely by changing the subject. "Sure am hungry. That pizza looks good."

"Pepperoni, sausage or cheese?" Molly poised near his shoulder, toting pie slices on paper plates, yellow-spotted with grease.

He reached up. His gentle tug on her elbow forced her to lean closer to him to balance the food. "Sorry," he said, enjoying her fresh, floral scent.

****

His smile transformed his features from handsome to stunning. Molly forced herself to be impervious even though his nearness shot another hormonal flash through her system.

He pointed to a slice of pepperoni pizza.

She handed him a full plate. "I accept your apology. Be a good patient from now on, and all is forgiven."

"Patient?" asked a mom.

"You're Molly's patient?" asked a woman on his right.

"Yes. Lucky, huh? Beautiful doctor and all." He bit into the pizza and tugged hard to break through the crust.

Molly sat down at the table, sampled her pizza and encountered the same difficulty. She tore a piece off the slice of pie with her fingers. "Your charm's thicker than this cardboard crust."

"Uncle Danny has a bullet hole in his neck," Mary imparted to her friends.

The little girls fired questions over each other.

"That's so cool. Did it hurt?"

"Do you have a gun? Did you shoot back?"

"Why would somebody shoot you?"

"Hey, Mom, is he a Humpty?"

Amy's question struck her as funny and Molly slapped a napkin in front of her mouth to keep from spraying food. "Yes, Amy," she managed to say. "Inside joke," she directed to the table at large.

"Detective Sullivan..." she swept her hand in Dan's direction.

"Detective-Lieutenant, actually," he corrected.

"Sorry," she arched an eyebrow at him. "Detective-Lieutenant Sullivan was injured in the line of duty last week and suffered a bullet wound to the shoulder. I headed the trauma team that treated him."

"It's nothing. I'm fine." He looked around the table. "How about those Sox? Or we could talk about something else."

"I have a question for you, Danny, since you're a policeman," one of the moms said. "Do you know anything about the Henna Housewife Murders?" she asked in a low voice, one eye trained on the kids' table.

He frowned. "Yes, I do." He leaned forward to keep the conversation from being overheard by the children. "The media reports have been accurate. The victims had dyed-red hair and were killed in suburban neighborhoods in broad daylight. We don't have solid leads yet, but my department is working around the clock to solve these murders."

He looked pointedly at Molly and raised the volume of his voice a notch, "And I would be doing the same thing if my doctor allowed me to go back to work."

She didn't take the bait. Instead she fussed around the children's table dishing out seconds.

Bobbie jumped up to help her, burnished red hair cascading down her back.

"Oh, Bobbie," Molly said. "Your hair."

"Don't worry, I've never dyed my hair in my life."

She grasped Bobbie's hand and led her back to the adult table. "Danny, are there any special precautions I can beg Bobbie to follow? Look at her red hair."

"You should be careful. That goes for everyone," Dan advised. "There's no such thing as being too cautious. Keep your doors and windows locked, *all* of them. Keep your car doors locked until you're inside a closed garage if you can. Avoid being alone, even during the day. Report anyone who looks out of place in your neighborhood, on foot, on a bike, on a motorcycle or in a car."

He took some frayed business cards out of his jeans pocket and handed them around the table. "Call this number if you have anything to report. Don't hesitate. I teach a self-defense course at the community college. I want you to sign up and tell your friends about it. The next class meets Tuesday morning. I'll give you simple techniques to discourage an attacker and buy yourself time to get away and get help."

He looked disgusted. "Correct that. My brother is teaching *my* self-defense course on a temporary basis. No medical release, no duty of any kind. All I need is your signature, Doc."

He stretched a dimpled smile in Molly's direction. It missed the mark in sincerity. She ignored him.

Bobbie looked at the card in her hand. "I think I'll take you up on the class, Detective Sullivan."

"That's a great idea, Bobbie," Molly said. "Thank you, Dan. Now to repay you, I'll drive you and Mary home in your car later, while Bobbie takes Amy home in mine."

"Hell if you will…"

She pressed her hand on his left arm, squeezing to drive home her point. "It's no trouble, Dan. Really. I wouldn't have it any other way."

After she organized cleanup, Molly looked around for Dan. He was gone. *Damn patients do whatever the hell they want.*

Chapter 5

Molly walked into her gleaming kitchen, eager for the first cup of coffee of the day. Rosy, sunrise light streamed through double windows over the sink and glinted off stainless steel and polished granite. Still in her robe, she had another half hour before she had to wake Amy to get ready for school.

Bobbie perched on a high stool at the center island and leaned over the morning newspaper. She turned the pages in wide, crackling arcs, sipped tea and scanned the headlines. It was unusual enough that she was dressed this early, but the thigh-hugging denim skirt and brocade jacket she wore were a big departure from her habitual, fitted sweat pants and little hooded tops.

She had taken time to put on makeup, too. A subtle foundation almost covered her freckles. Her honey-colored eyes popped with charcoal liner and a brush of mascara. Her waist-length, red hair fell in waves down her back. The gleaming strands caught the early morning sunlight and reflected a soft auburn wash of color against the gold tones in her jacket.

Molly pushed the button on the coffee maker

and leaned back against the counter, legs angled. "You look terrific. And you're up early, too. Going somewhere?"

"I have school this morning. I signed up for the self-defense class at the community college that Dan told us about at the party. I think all the stay-at-home moms have signed up, too. He was pretty persuasive. I guess he has to be."

Bobbie hung over the newspaper. "There was another attack. Another woman is dead. I can't believe it." She pointed to a line of print. "It says right here, this monster only targets red-haired housewives."

Molly shook her head. "This is creeping me out, thinking about you alone so much during the day."

"Me, too." Bobbie scanned the article again. "It doesn't say anything about dyed hair in this article. Just red hair. Makes me nervous."

She mashed the newspaper closed, folded it several times and pushed it aside. "Of course, over and over, the media repeats their catchy name for him. We need to know about this, but I'm already tired of hearing 'The Henna Housewife Killer'."

"I know. Makes me sneer at the TV every time I hear it." Molly watched the coffee carafe fill by drips, a mug in her left hand and the pot handle in her right.

"I think it's a great idea for you to take the class. You can't hide that head of hair, and it can't be a coincidence that all the victims had the same hair color."

Molly poured her coffee and slid onto a stool next to Bobbie. She cupped her hands around the ceramic mug and took a tentative sip of the steaming brew. She sighed with pleasure and unfolded the paper to find the article Bobbie had been reading. "Does it say anything in the article about how the attacks occur?" She flipped pages.

"It's pretty vague." Bobbie put her arm around Molly's shoulder. "But I don't want you to worry about me. I'm always cautious. This class will teach me how to protect myself."

Molly didn't want to think about someone she loved being at risk for violence again. She looked at Bobbie, so dear to her. *Please, God, keep her safe.*

"You really do look pretty. Is that makeup you're wearing?"

Bobbie swiveled in her seat and faced Molly. "Okay, Mol. I knew you'd wonder why I'm all dolled up. You can practically read my mind. I want to look nice for my teacher. If he looks half as good as his brother…yummy."

"Yummy? Don't be ridiculous. Dan Sullivan might be a lot of things—conceited, pig-headed, stubborn, and exasperating come to mind. But, yummy? I don't think so."

"He might have all those bad qualities, Doc, but you have to admit that he is one delicious specimen. Don't you just want to bite him?"

Molly laughed. Bobbie often read her mind, too. She did want to take a bite out of Dan, but she wouldn't admit it. "I didn't really notice him that much."

"Really? Well, you were the only female at the rink that didn't. Even the ancient babe handing out the skates made lip-smacking noises as he walked past."

"I had more fun things to do at the rink than drool over a stubborn, egotistical male."

Molly stood to end the conversation. "Be careful today, Bobbie. Will you please call me after your class to let me know how it went?"

"I will, Mol. Don't worry. I promise to be a good student. Maybe tonight I'll have some moves to teach you."

****

Bobbie parked the jeep in the crowded parking lot and hurried between two long rows of cars into the main building on the campus. She decided to go in early instead of wasting time sitting in the car. She was glad she did.

Only a few seats were open in the back rows of desks. She chose one by the window so she could chat with the mothers she knew. A cluster of talkative white-haired women took up the first two rows. Their louder voices made a racket in the stadium-like lecture hall.

Conversations ended in succession when a man in khaki slacks and a navy blue crewneck sweater walked in. His arms outstretched beneath a cardboard box, he made his way down each carpeted step to the front of the room. His eyes widened as he descended. He looked nervous. His resemblance to Dan Sullivan was unmistakable and Bobbie was glad she took some extra time getting ready that morning. Dan's brother was yummy.

She understood why the women around her sat straighter in their chairs and smiled at the sight of him. *My goodness, the Sullivan brothers are handsome devils.*

****

He set the box down on the "teacher's" desk, swallowed and faced the sea of women. "Good morning, ladies. My name is Joe Sullivan. You were probably expecting my brother, Dan."

"Where is Dan, dear?" asked one of the front row, senior citizens.

"Is he all right?" asked another.

"It is not like him to miss class," a third pronounced.

Dan had forewarned him about the senior brigade. They took the front rows in his class every session, despite the fact that this was a one-session course. They treated him as if he were their

44

grandson. They considered it their responsibility to critique each class and give helpful hints to him afterward about his presentation style, the course content and whether or not they liked his haircut or clothes that day. Dan loved these feisty, little ladies and expected him to treat them well.

"Dan is fine. He had a little accident. He's under strict doctor's orders to rest. He'll be back next month," Joe advised them.

"Is it true that he was shot?" called out the apparent leader of the brigade. "I wouldn't call being shot a little accident."

Joe ran a hand over his brow. Dan didn't want him to go into detail about his condition. But these ladies obviously cared about his brother. "It is true that he was shot, but he received excellent medical treatment and he's recovering nicely. He's already driving everyone crazy, balking at the enforced leave. I promise you, he'll be back soon."

"Now ladies, let's get down to business. I want each one of you to leave this classroom today feeling strong and angry and powerful."

****

Joe started out shaky, but he became more authoritative and confident as he lectured.

Bobbie gazed at him as he stood, legs shoulder length apart. His hands were folded behind his back. The stance accentuated the v-shape of his torso. He smiled at her several times making her feel singled out and special.

"Men attack and rape almost 400,000 women every year in America," he said. "That's a good reason to feel fearful. But I'm not giving you this statistic to frighten you. You have the power to take control of the situation if you are attacked. I don't want you to be afraid. Today I'll give you the tools you need to feel empowered and in control."

He pulled a bottle of water from the box on his

45

desk, unscrewed its cap and paced. "I'm sure you know there's an attacker loose in the area and I assume it's one of the reasons you're here today. How do you protect yourself from him or any other attacker? What should you do if someone comes up behind you?"

He took a sip of water and stood ramrod straight in front of the group. "Use your head. I mean that two ways. Stay calm. Think. If you're grabbed from behind, don't waste your time trying to step on your attacker's toes, or flail your legs around trying to kick him. The human skull is a powerful weapon. Use it to bash his face. You have to be angry, not afraid. If you're attacked, is losing an option? No! This is one fight you have to win no matter what."

The man and his message absorbed Bobbie. Not only impressive to look at, he was passionate about equipping every woman in the class to keep safe.

"I see the questioning looks on your faces," he went on. "You're wondering if you would be able to overpower someone stronger and bigger. Ladies, I want you to remember one thing. Size does not matter."

He smiled in response to a smattering of giggles from the audience. "Uh, that's not to say." His face reddened. "I mean..."

What a sweet man.

He cleared his throat and plowed on. "Your attacker will pick you and try to make you a victim because he sees you as vulnerable. Don't let him. Scream. Yell at the top of your lungs. Every part of your body can be used as a weapon when used forcefully. Use your fingers to gouge his eyes. Use your elbows to pound him. Fight ladies, fight."

He chose volunteers to demonstrate movements. Even the senior brigade got in the act and they used their bony elbows to pummel him with gleeful zeal. He'd have a few bruises to show for his teaching skill. The hour allotted for the course seemed to pass in a few minutes.

When class ended, the women lined up to speak with Joe. He gave each one a packet of handouts and diagrams of different self-defense movements to practice. The women praised him. The seniors gave him their ultimate tribute. They gushed over him and told him he taught the class as well as his brother. Dan would not be disappointed with him, they promised.

Bobbie, last in line, waited her turn. She felt drawn to Joe.

When she reached the desk she extended her hand. "Hi. I'm Bobbie Leighton. What a great class. I didn't expect it to be so powerful. I do feel angry and strong now."

He shook her hand. "Thank you for saying that. That's exactly what I wanted you all to feel."

"You succeeded. You're a great teacher. Your brother should worry that you'll take over his class."

"No way. I almost turned tail and ran when I saw everyone staring at me. Trust me. I wanted to kill my brother for getting me into this."

"How is Dan, really?"

"He really is fine. Driving my family nuts. We all can't wait until he's released for active duty. I think he's at the hospital now convincing my brother-in-law, Mike, to spring him." He frowned. "Do you know Dan?"

"I met him at the skating rink with Mary. I'm sure you know Amy, Mary's twin by different parents?" She laughed.

"Of course I know Amy. She's become part of our family."

"I take care of Amy. I've been with the Jordans since Amy was born. When Molly moved here after her husband died, I moved with her."

"Dr. Molly Jordan? That's how you know Dan."

47

"I don't really know him. I just met him once. He looked a little weak at Amy's party. And seemed to be interested in my boss."

Joe looked happier. He plucked his suit jacket from the back of the desk chair and slipped it on. They left the classroom together and walked outside until they reached Bobbie's car. She waited while Joe opened the door for her.

"Nice to meet you, Bobbie. I hope we see each other again sometime."

She beamed up at him as he closed the car door. "Nice meeting you, too. See you."

He shifted on his feet and looked like he had something more to say. Bobbie waved and backed out of the parking space.

In her rear view mirror, as she pulled out of the parking lot, she noticed that he watched her leave. *Hmmm. Officer, I certainly hope our paths cross again real soon.*

Exhilarated, she decided to visit the hospital and surprise Molly with lunch. She could reassure her boss that she felt better able to protect herself. And she'd make sure Molly ate something decent for a change. She pulled into a space near the local sandwich shop and picked up two veggie wraps and some fresh fruit salad.

At the hospital, she stopped at the administrative desk in the trauma center. She was the only person who stood in one spot. It was bedlam. Trudy swung out of one of the exam rooms and reversed direction when she saw Bobbie wave.

"Hi, Trudy. Do you know where Doc is?"

"Hey, Bobbie. You're in luck. She's taking a break. We've been slammed this morning. We had a lull and I convinced her to go to the staff lounge to get off her feet for while."

"Thanks. I know how to get to the lounge."

Bobbie walked through the circular hall that

skirted the exam rooms and averted her eyes so that she didn't see anything that made her too squeamish to eat. A wide corridor connected the satellite trauma center building to the main hospital. She passed through that corridor, turned right and headed towards a door marked "Hospital Staff Only."

She pulled the door open and looked around inside before she stepped in. Molly sat alone on a couch, her eyes closed, in the large, bright room. Her natural skin color, fair and clear warmed with peach overtones, looked yellowish blue in the harsh florescent light.

Cheap, faux-leather furniture and a collection of mismatched, armless chairs with chrome-plated legs, sprawled in haphazard groupings around the rectangular room. The gray and white-flecked linoleum, though old, shone spotless.

Molly opened her eyes at the sound of the door latch. When she saw Bobbie, her eyes snapped wide with alarm.

"Hi Doc. Don't worry. Everything's fine at home. I brought lunch."

"Oh." Molly sighed. "What a wonderful surprise. I'm starved and was about to raid the vending machine. Must have dozed off, though."

She peeked in the white paper bag Bobbie set on the coffee table in front of her. "How did class go?"

"It was very interesting. I learned a lot, including that the other Sullivan brother is as delicious as the first."

"I know. I met Joe the same day Dan was wounded."

Once the words were out of her mouth, Molly realized she made an inadvertent admission that Dan was delicious. Bobbie had that moony, I'm-about-to-fall-in-love-again look on her face. *Maybe she won't notice.*

"I hope I get to see Joe again soon. He's a great teacher. The class loved him. I have so much to show you tonight."

Before Molly could maneuver the conversation away from either Sullivan brother, delicious Dan followed Mike Lynch into the staff lounge. Molly may have groaned aloud. She remained determined not to get entangled with a cop again, especially a maddening, egotistical cop, and yet Dan kept appearing in her world to tempt her.

Molly enjoyed working with Mike Lynch, a brilliant surgeon with national ranking. She appreciated his diplomacy and availability because of her department's constant need for surgical services. He would come to her whenever she asked him. She would not have asked him to come see her with Dan in tow.

"Hi, Molly. I hear you were swamped today," Mike said.

"Swamped sounds like a nice, peaceful drowning," she replied. "Today it's more like we were steamrolled. Is there, by chance, a full moon tonight?"

"Always a full moon in the ER." Mike smiled and gestured toward Dan. "This is my brother-in-law, Danny. Danny, this is Molly Jordan, our best ER attending physician."

The skin prickled on her arms with Dan's nearness. He stood next to Mike, which served to emphasize his superior physique, and accelerate Molly's pulse. She forced a smile.

"We've already met, Mike," she said in a neutral tone. "Hello, Dan."

"Good to see you, Molly."

They shook hands. She worked to keep her face expressionless. Inside, she suppressed a shudder of pleasure.

"I signed Dan's medical release today," Mike

said. "Now he can stop driving us all crazy and go back to work and drive criminals crazy instead."

Mike's beeper went off. He pulled it off his belt and glanced at it. "I have to go. Catch you later." He stepped backward towards the door. "Dan, don't do anything stupid. Okay? Take it easy. I don't want to have to explain to your sister that I let you go back to work too soon." Mike hurried out the door.

"I promise, I'll be good," Dan said to Mike's back.

His green eyes danced with roguish charm. Molly found it hard to keep that shudder repressed.

He didn't let go of her hand until he turned to speak to Bobbie. "Hi, Bobbie. Good to see you again, too."

"Same here, Dan. I was just telling Molly about the self- defense class I took this morning with Joe. He was great. I really enjoyed the class."

"I'm glad." Dan glanced at the open bag on the coffee table. "Am I interrupting lunch?"

"No, not at all," Bobbie said, "more like just in time for lunch." She inched towards the door. "I have to run."

"You didn't even eat." Molly rummaged inside the bag. "And there are two wraps in here."

"I just wanted to drop off your lunch. I have some errands to run before I get Amy from school. Nice seeing you again, Dan."

She left Dan and Molly alone.

Chapter 6

Molly crossed her arms beneath her breasts and leaned back into the stiff sofa.

"So you managed to strong-arm Mike." Her tone dripped with disapproval. "Three weeks isn't enough time after the injury you sustained. I wouldn't have signed those release papers if you'd have come to me."

She propped her legs on the coffee table and crossed her ankles. "But you got your˙ mission accomplished by going around me. Bye, Dan. Stay healthy."

He ignored the brush-off. "Yep, it's official. I can go back to work now."

He swung an arm to grab a rickety chair and took a seat in front of her. "Mind if I join you for lunch? You mentioned there are two sandwiches in that bag?"

"Good thing, too. Boy, am I hungry." Get lost was written all over her face.

It challenged him. "I have a lot of work to do and I want to get back to the station and wave these release papers in my captain's face, but I can always find time for a pretty lady like you."

He smiled, having fun. She gritted her teeth and didn't smile back.

"You're angry with me." He kept his tone even, which had the desired effect of making her defensive.

"No, I'm not." She unfolded her arms and leaned forward. "I'm frustrated. I was right at Amy's party. You shouldn't have been driving or skating. You could have hurt yourself. And you're taking an unnecessary risk to go back to police work before you're healed. What if your reflexes are just a second off? What if...?" She swallowed hard.

"I won't get hurt," he said gently. "Nothing's going to happen to me." He searched her eyes.

She lowered her eyes and a pink tinge colored her cheeks. "Sorry. It's none of my business now, anyway. You've got your release." She resumed her get-out-of-here posture on the couch.

He ignored the second brush-off, grabbed a sandwich and leaned back in the chair. "Got something against cops?"

"Of course not." She picked up the other sandwich and looked at her pager as if willing it to beep. She ate and refused to meet his eyes, food the excuse not to speak.

Dan chewed, relaxed and thoughtful. He filled his belly with food and filled his senses with the sight and smell of this enigmatic female. She smelled like spring lilacs in his mother's yard, and looked like a temptress despite the shapeless lab coat that couldn't hide the soft curves of her breasts or the cinch of her tiny waist. Her hair gleamed, even in the unflattering light, and capped her head with messy silken spikes he wanted to sink his hands in as he angled her head back for a kiss.

Adept at reading body language, he picked up mixed signals. He was captivated by the contradiction of her apparent concern and her intent to get rid of him. *She's just as attracted to me as I am to her.*

He chose an innocuous subject to get her talking. "I'm glad Bobbie enjoyed the class this morning. Joe was a bundle of nerves. Teaching is not his thing."

"Sounds to me like he did a good job. I'm so worried that she could be a target for this maniac."

"One of the main reasons I want to get back to work is to stop this guy. Or the HH Killer as the press calls him." He huffed, disgusted. "Watching the investigation from the sidelines is not my style. Luckily, my brothers have kept me informed."

"Brothers, plural?"

"Yes, all my brothers have been following this case closely."

"How many brothers do you have?"

"Four. I'm the oldest. You apparently met Joe at the hospital? He gushes about what a good doctor you are."

She flashed him a self-satisfied smile like a queen on her Naugahyde throne to her lowly subject.

"Don't let it go to your head," he said, laughing. "Brian works homicide, too. Patrick is a federal investigator with ATF, and the baby, Jimmy, just graduated from the academy."

"Good God. How does your mother handle worrying about five children in harm's way?"

"Used to be six, plus the love of her life. Kay was Chicago PD before she got pregnant with Mary. Dad just retired his job as Commissioner a few years ago after forty years on the force."

"Your poor mother. How could she sleep nights with your dad on the force for forty years and all her children following in his footsteps? She must have nightmares."

"She knows we're well trained and capable of handling ourselves. And she knows that when your time is up, your time is up. She's a very sensible woman," he said.

"A sensible woman would have the sense to worry. Sometimes being well trained and capable of handling yourself isn't enough." She pushed her half-eaten sandwich aside.

"Why do I get the feeling we're not talking about my mother or my family?"

"I'm sorry. I don't know why I said anything." The color drained from her face and she rubbed her arms with her hands. She shivered. She looked furious, why, Dan wasn't sure. She met his eyes. A thin sheen of tears rimmed her lake-blue eyes, pain shimmering in their depths.

"I'm sorry, Molly." He hurtled the coffee table, sat next to her and reached his arm over her shoulders. "I didn't mean to make you cry. What did I do?"

"It's not you. You didn't do anything. It's me."

She sighed and dragged her hand through her hair. "I was married to an NYPD cop. I was scared every day with Eddie that something would happen to him. Every single day when he walked out the door, I couldn't shake the thought that he might not come home and that I might never see him again. A little piece of me died every time he headed off to work. I don't know how your mother could face that every day for more than forty years."

Tears spilled and ran narrow tracks down both her cheeks.

He didn't want to make her cry in the first place and he was sure the next question would make it worse, but he wanted to try to understand. "And what you dreaded happened, didn't it?"

"Of course, it did." Her voice was a monotone. "He survived 911. Can you believe that? He was right there when it happened. He pulled people from the devastation. Didn't hurt a hair on his head."

Dan shook his head, able to envision what it was like.

"Eddie was killed in an attempted liquor store robbery by a fifteen-year-old. He wasn't even on duty. He stopped on his day off to pick up a bottle of wine for us to have with dinner. Senseless. I was on the staff of the ER where they brought him, but I wasn't on duty. They wouldn't have let me work on him anyway. At least I got there in time to hold him and say goodbye."

Dan tightened his arm around her shoulders and she leaned her head against his chest. His brand of sympathy was expressed with silence and a hug. He could never find handy words to wrap around grief. No one had ever helped assuage his grief with words. His own grief could fill him with rage, if he let himself go there.

His wife never worried about him every day when he left for work. She was too busy screwing that guy at her office. She said women wanted a nine-to-five husband. Didn't hurt that he drove a Benz and had a fat bank account, either. When the divorce was final, he thought the grief would kill him. But there were plenty of arms in the Sullivan family and plenty of unspoken words of sympathy.

It was easy to find refuge in work. The job could consume you and he let it. He thought he knew what he wanted when he got married — sharing everyday life with someone who wanted the same things. What he wanted since his divorce was to avoid falling into the same trap again.

Chapter 7

Molly emerged from the thrall of her painful memories aware of the muted drum of Dan's heartbeat and the clean, citrus scent of his aftershave. She raised her head off his chest. Exposed and mortified by her display of raw emotion, she wanted to get away from him now more than ever or lay her head back down over his heart and let the quickening inside her take over her senses.

"I'm so sorry, Molly, for your loss, and Amy's," he said.

His compassion eased her embarrassment. Strange, that a fellow cop could understand the unrelenting fear she lived with as a cop's wife. Eddie never did, and he had insisted she worried for nothing. Dan's assurance affirmed she was right.

"You're wrong," were the next words out of Dan's mouth. "He didn't die because he was a cop. He died because it was his time. There's no reason to worry about something that's out of our hands. My parents always had that philosophy and it makes perfect sense to me. Simple."

"Don't tell me I'm wrong, Dan Sullivan. There's

nothing simple about death," she exclaimed. "Eddie thought that he was Superman, that he was invincible. He should have worried. It might have saved him."

He brushed his hand lightly on her arm and didn't react when she flinched. "He *was* Superman, Molly. Until it was his time."

Molly couldn't mount a solid argument against fate. The heat of argument dissipated and she sat with Dan's arm casually draped around her. He wasn't afraid to stand up to her. *Unbelievable. I actually like this man.*

"What about you, Danny? Do you think you're Superman?"

"Sure, I do." He wadded up a sandwich wrapper and sunk it dead center in a wastebasket across the room. "Superman." He made a muscle, elbow pointed at Molly.

She snorted. "More like Clark Kent, lying in my ER with a bullet hole in you, muscle man." She stood up.

"Guy must have had kryptonite in his pocket."

He stood next to her and she felt small and vulnerable. The heft of him, his clean male smell, the radiating warmth from his body made her tilt into a slight lean towards him. *Bobbie, I'll take that bite now.*

She straightened, gathered the remaining lunch refuse, including the untouched fruit salad, and tossed it. There were limits to how much healthy food she felt like eating. And limits to where she'd let her libido take her with delicious Dan.

The undercurrent pulled between them. His knowing grin set Molly's nerves thrumming. She would not let this cocky male get to her. She managed a casual smile. "Still don't know how your mom handles the likes of you."

"She keeps all the Sullivans in line. Truth is,

we're all afraid of her."

They laughed together, all tensions between them at bay for the moment.

"I better go," Dan told her. "I want to get up to speed at work."

"Me, too. I'm surprised I had this long for lunch. After the morning I had, it's almost a miracle."

They moved towards the door.

"Mary asked me this morning if I would take her to see the latest Harry Potter movie this weekend," he said. "Would you and Amy like to come along?"

That sounds innocent enough. And touching he'd spend time with kids. "Amy would love to go. She's a Potter groupie."

"Great. How about Friday night?"

"I'm on call. How about Saturday night?"

"No, I'll be back on duty. Does Sunday work?"

"Sorry, I'm on call Sunday, too."

"Would it be okay if I take Amy on Friday night? I really don't want to disappoint Mary."

"I'm sure Amy would love that, if you don't mind."

"I don't mind at all. Maybe I could have a rain check with her mother?"

"Maybe." Superman or no Superman, blood pressure spikes from his touch or not, Molly wouldn't get tangled up with Dan. She'd just be asking for trouble.

He strode into the hall and she followed him. Bobbie barreled into the two of them on a full run.

Panting, Bobbie grabbed Molly's wrist. "Mol you have to come back to the ER. I think I broke his nose. There was blood everywhere. I didn't mean to break it."

"Slow down. Tell me what happened. Are you all right?" She looked with dismay at the bloodstains splotching Bobbie's clothes.

"I'm fine, but I don't think Joe is. I think I broke

his nose."

"Joe who?" Molly asked.

"Joe Sullivan."

"My brother? You broke my brother's nose? Oh, this is rich." Dan's laughter exploded, even though Molly's stiff posture should have clued him that she didn't think this was a laughing matter.

"Yes, your stupid brother. It was all his fault." Frantic, Bobbie pushed them both forward and led them on a half-run into the long corridor back toward the ER.

Molly double-stepped to flank Bobbie. "Tell me exactly what happened."

"Okay." Bobbie linked arms with Molly and they walked in sync. "I went out to my car and was just about to open the door when someone came up behind me and put his arms around me. The first thing I thought of was what Joe taught us in class. I got mad and I used my head as a weapon. I smashed it back as hard as I could. I didn't know it was Joe. How stupid of him to come up behind me like that after teaching me how to defend myself."

Dan was prudent enough not to say anything.

As they reached the perimeter hall of the ER, Dr. Jordan took charge. "You both stay out here. I'll check on Joe and let you know what I find. Calm down, Bobbie. You should be happy that you know how to defend yourself. I'm proud of you."

It took Molly two minutes, although it probably felt longer to Joe, to set the clean break in his nose. After she packed his nostrils with cotton, and had a nurse swab some of the dried blood off his face and neck, Molly let Dan and Bobbie into the exam room. Joe sat on a gurney and his legs dangled over the side. White adhesive tape covered his nose. His eyes were already blackening.

"Don't say a thing, Dan. I mean it." Joe glared and looked as ferocious as a panda.

As if Dan could resist. "You should be proud, bro. You did a bang-up job as a self-defense teacher. Drove your point home."

Dan walked over to Joe and probed the bridge of his nose with his fingers.

"Ow." Joe shot Dan a murderous look.

"And Bobbie drove your point straight into your skull." Dan cackled like a schoolboy.

"You idiots." Molly pushed Dan aside and shone a penlight into each of Joe's eyes. "Someone will need to wake you every hour for the next twenty-four hours. You might be concussed."

"I'm so sorry, Joe." Bobbie looked miserable. "Oh, look at your eyes. I can't tell you how sorry I am."

"Don't be. It was my fault. When I came here to check on Dan, I was surprised to see you by your car." Joe touch-tested around his nose and brought his hand away from his face with a low grunt.

His voice sounded like he held his nose. "I enjoyed meeting you this morning and thought I'd ask you if you wanted to grab some lunch. Then I decided to come up behind you like we talked about in class and see how you handled it."

"A regular pop quiz. A+ for Bobbie." Dan could not be contained.

Molly swatted him on the back. He put his arms up in mock self-defense and laughed again. It was contagious and caught Molly up, too. Dan's eyes watered and Molly giggled with him, the two suspended in the moment as if nobody else were in the room.

Molly sobered when the reality of Bobbie's stricken expression and Joe's bashed face penetrated. She swatted Dan again.

"Enough." She smoothed the lapels of her jacket. "Dan, take your brother home."

"Come on, little bro." Dan put a tender arm

around Joe's shoulder for support as Joe slid off the gurney. "I'll take you to Mama's and she can fix you some nice chicken soup."

"I'll…" Bobbie said. "I'll walk you to the car. I wish I could somehow make amends. I could bring you some chicken soup."

"You two go ahead." Dan steadied Joe on his feet before he let go of him. "I'll be right there."

"When the brothers hear about this, there will be no living it down." Dan smiled at Molly.

"Poor Joe." Her beeper went off. She checked the digital read-out on the device. "Back to work. I don't think you have to worry that your self-defense class was short-changed in your absence."

"True."

They walked out of the exam room together.

"I don't think you have to worry about Bobbie. She can take care of herself." He walked away from her, whistling the Chicago Bears fight song.

She watched him leave, all swagger and virility. It didn't change the fact that he was still only about seventy-five percent healed. In her opinion.

At the admin desk she hesitated a few seconds over the telephone console before placing a call to Dan's captain.

Chapter 8

Danny strode into the station house and the familiar professional connection clicked inside him. He had hungered to be back for weeks. Too much had been going on for him to tolerate inaction while the HH investigation floundered. Invigorated, he was ready to cast a fresh eye on what meager evidence they'd gathered.

Relieved that he could put his injury in the past, he ignored the stiff arm that still throbbed like a toothache from his neck to his fingertips.

Danny tapped his knuckles on the open office door, walked over and placed the medical release papers on his captain's desk. He stretched out his hand to his superior officer.

Captain Tony Caprisi rose from his seat, clasped Danny's hand and gave it an enthusiastic shake. "Good to see you, Danny. Have a seat."

"Good to see you, too, Captain. Glad to be back. Can't stand being inactive for so long. I'm pretty much up to speed on the high priority investigation. I've been picking Joe's brain during my leave. I want to review the files. Keep feeling like I'm missing something."

Caprisi walked around the desk and perched one hip over its front corner. "Good idea. I want you to stay on the desk for a couple weeks." He looked over at Danny placidly.

"Couple weeks? I'll only need a couple hours. I'm fit, Captain, and ready for active duty. The doc signed the medical release." Danny pointed to the paperwork on the desk.

"Kay's husband signed the release. I'd say that's unofficial." Caprisi looked at him evenly.

"What are you getting at? Mike's a licensed doctor."

"Had a call from the hospital a while ago. The attending physician said you needed to heal a minimum of two more weeks before going active. You can run the investigation from the desk until then or not at all." He stood, walked around his desk and took his chair.

Danny fought to keep his composure at the apparent dismissal. "What doctor? There must be some mistake. I'm going by the book here. The papers are in order. I'll get this…"

"Captain." A rookie rushed into the office. "Begging your pardon…hello Lieutenant Sullivan… We've got something on the horn. Looks like it's HH. Barnes is heading to the scene."

Danny sprang upright from the rush of adrenaline.

"Stay where you are, Sullivan."

The two men stared each other down. In the military-like hierarchy of Danny's career, he'd lose the contest. Orders were orders.

"Call in Joe. Where is he, Dan?"

"His place. Broken nose."

"Call him in."

The rookie pivoted and left to do the Captain's bidding.

Danny swallowed his frustration. He needed a

clear head to direct Joe. "I'll walk him through when he gets to the scene."

Danny turned away from the Captain and then reversed. "Who called from the hospital?"

Caprisi opened a drawer and pulled out a file — Danny's personnel file. He referred to a phone message slip inside the folder. "Doctor Molly Jordan, Trauma Center, Attending." He flipped the file closed.

"Okay. Thanks." He headed for the phone and dialed Joe. He'd deal with Doctor Molly Jordan in good time.

He waited to patch through and scanned his desk. *What the hell? Where is everything?*

Hadn't seen this dog-eared blotter for months. And that was the way he liked it. A full, fake-leather pencil cup with the department's insignia on it was positioned a precise inch off the right corner of the blotter and a family picture matched the distance off the left corner. *Shit. All it needed was a nice vase of flowers.*

Cradling the phone on his shoulder, a knife-jab of pain scissored down his arm. He shifted the phone to the other side, yanked his file drawer open and didn't recognize the contents.

An even row of Pendaflex folders hung around bulging case files. Plastic inserts housed tab cards with typed case numbers on them. The files were arranged in case number sequence from the lowest to the highest. They were his cases—that much was familiar.

So stupefied at the condition of his desk, he didn't bother to try to sort out the apparent color-coordinated scheme of the file labels, also typed.

Joe's nasal-sounding voice cut through the white air in his ear.

"Danny. I just got to the scene. Techies are already working and from the looks of it, I have

65

some crowd control to do."

"What the hell have you done to my desk, you anal bastard?"

"What?"

"Never mind. Describe what you see." He heard background voices and the thud of a car door.

"Tape's up around the driveway leading to the garage. It's one of those quad homes. Driveway for the unit curves around the side and garage opens to the back of the property. Can't see it from the street."

Dan heard nothing but ambient noise and footsteps for several seconds.

"Same MO. Vic is still in the trunk. Late thirties, early forties I'd say. Red hair. Long. Hold on."

Danny listened to jumbled voices but couldn't make out more than a few scattered words. He scanned the folders in his drawer and plucked up several with his right hand. He grimaced as the slight physical exertion drilled a cascade of pain into the right side of his neck. *Damn. He softened his attitude toward Molly Jordan's meddling a couple degrees.*

"The ME is here. TOD approximately eleven hundred. Slash across the throat. Cross slashes on both eyes. Puncture wounds in the torso. Broken bag and spilled food on the garage floor. More bags in the trunk under the body."

"Walk the perimeter. Are you walking the perimeter?"

"Yea. Keep your shirt on. I know what I'm doing."

"Matter of opinion."

"Don't get nasty, bro."

"Yea, sorry." Danny bobbled a drumbeat on the floor with his leg. He itched to be walking the perimeter of the scene with his brother. He wanted to see it, feel it, smell it, and poke at it with all his senses.

"Anything seem out of place?"

"No. Grass is pretty dry. No footprints on the lawn from what I can see. I think he waltzed right up the driveway."

Dan sat on the edge of his seat and pushed forward with each aggressive question trying to will some decent evidence out of the crime scene. "What else do you see?"

"Not much. Give me a break, Danny."

"Yea, sorry."

Danny heard the blat of a walkie-talkie and Joe's clipped response.

"I've got neighbors to contend with. And the press is here. Christ, I feel like my nose was drilled into my brain."

Danny chuckled. "Yea, well it was. Bested by a girl."

"A pretty girl. At least I drew the sympathy card. I'll play it when the pounding in my head stops. Gotta go, Danny. I'll brief you as soon as I can get back there."

"Don't forget to canvas the neighborhood. And check out the grocery store…"

"I've got it, Danny."

"Don't let the press near the body."

"Jesus, Dan."

"Okay, okay. I'll see you later. Thanks, Joe."

"Sure."

Danny picked up a folder and spread it open on his desk. Stark photos of nearly the same scene Joe had just described spilled out. He didn't need to open the other two folders on his desk to know he'd see virtually the same shots.

But he did open the folders and stare at the photographs, not just to get inside the killer's head somehow, but also to treat each victim with individual concern and respect.

The murders looked the same but they weren't. The same person was the perpetrator; he was sure of that. But each victim, each woman, had been very different and had her own special life until the killer took it away. The only way he could honor the victims was to focus on their murderer until he could make the evidence add up to the magic answer. Who was the HH Killer?

Chapter 9

Molly's Tylenol-defiant headache mushroomed from mere nuisance to pounding bass drums. She steered the jeep down the narrow, unpaved access road and created a dust storm that filmed her windshield with brown grit. The phrase "out in the sticks" took on new meaning as overhanging tree limbs assaulted the car on both sides. The brittle sounds of cracking branches and tires churning up gravel filled the car as they left a trail of sticks behind them.

"Do you think this is the right road, Amy?" Molly squinted ahead and kept both hands on the steering wheel.

"I think so, Mom." Amy consulted a sheet of printed directions spread on her lap. "The sign on the road said 'Deer Lake Camp' and the arrow pointed this way."

Molly prayed she wouldn't encounter a car going in the opposite direction. Unless it could plow straight over the jeep, there was no way to let it pass. They pushed forward until they reached a small clearing.

SUVs, trucks and a mammoth, black Hummer

were parked in a neat row on a gravel lot. On a rise ahead, Molly saw the backs of several, tiny log cabins, weathered black-brown.

Amy seemed revived from her six-hour ride funk. Vibrations of little girl energy orbited her as she grabbed their gear from the trunk. The bass drums kicked up a notch.

"We're in cabin number ten, Momma," Amy said, her voice joyful. She tore up the hill ahead of Molly.

"I'm right behind you." Molly slung a duffel bag over her shoulder and lugged a rolled sleeping bag in each hand.

At the last minute, while she had packed that morning, she threw a bottle of wine into the duffel. Kay wouldn't want to drink any wine that evening because of her pregnancy, but maybe some of the other mothers would. Molly had the feeling that she would need wine at the end of the day. *Camping could be more than marshmallows on sticks and mosquito bites, couldn't it?*

As she reached the top of the rise, the vista opened. A dozen cabins perched in a half-moon arc on the crest of the hill. Acres of mown grass sloped in a pie-shaped apron to the shores of Deer Lake. The forest loomed on the right and left boundaries of the campgrounds, casting long silhouettes on the expanse of lawn and mirrored reflections on blue lake water.

Molly's spirits lifted and her headache abated as she drank in the pristine view and the pine-scented air.

Amy's squad had earned the camping trip for outselling all the other Charity girls in their cookie campaign. Molly thought the term, "reward camping trip," was an oxymoron and had been lukewarm at best about going. But maybe this outing would be fun after all.

She climbed two wooden steps that led to the

front of cabin ten, arms aching. Amy and Mary shoved out the cabin door, smiled hello to Molly and raced off together. She turned around to hold the door open with her back and let herself in. She swiveled forward just in time to see Dan Sullivan step out of his jeans in front of her.

"Uh...Dan?" Molly turned her back to him, cheeks burning, bass drums moving from her head to her chest. "What are you doing here?"

He walked in front of her in his underwear and planted hairy legs in her path. "Kay's still morning sick and Mike is on call this weekend. My other sibs ran for the hills when Kay called around for substitutes. I was the one she nabbed. I'm the only one in the family who has a desk job."

She stood looking at the floor, the weight of the duffel listing her to the left, the sleeping bags dragging at her sides. In a moment of guilt, she wanted to apologize to him for ratting him out to his captain and delaying his return to active duty.

"What's the matter, Molly? You shy around a man without his pants?"

The guilty feeling dissipated with his sarcasm. "No, you ape."

She shoved past him and threw her stuff on the lower of two wall bunks on one side of the room. "I'm trying to respect your privacy. I see modesty isn't your strong point. Do you have any idea how many men I've seen in skivvies? I'm not impressed."

He put two thumbs in the waistband of his briefs. "Maybe if I take these off."

Her heart lurched. "Funny. Put your pants on before my daughter comes back in here."

"Yes, ma'am." She couldn't miss the sarcastic inflection.

He grabbed a pair of shorts out of a duffel bag on his side of the room and pulled them on.

She hoisted a sleeping bag on the top and lower

bunks on her apparent side then turned to face him. "Just out of curiosity, why the hell did you agree to do this? Aren't you the only man here?"

"Nope, there are other fathers here." The color of his eyes changed from a misty green to a sooty moss. "But none of them in a cabin with an impossible woman."

"Is this even *allowed*?"

"Sure it is. We've got built-in chaperones."

He ignored the ladder's existence and pulled himself up to sit on his top bunk with one fluid, muscular flex of his arms. She trained her eye on his shoulders and detected the slightest imbalance in how he used his right arm.

He sat above her and his head almost touched the cabin's ceiling. Reflected light brought out the sheen of his long, black hair and played shadows across his face that made him look mysterious and dangerous. His long, powerful legs dangled off the bunk.

Beneath him, she felt the small room shrink around them. In the cramped space she was tempted to move toward him to run her hands up his calves and thighs, and sample the feel of sinewy muscle and silky hair beneath her fingers. She wanted just a touch. She needed some air.

He looked down at her with a scowl on his face. Her reverie ended.

"I can't stay overnight in this cabin with you," she said curtly. "It's not right. What kind of example is this for Amy? I have to talk to somebody and get this changed..."

"Relax." He vaulted off the bunk and landed like a two hundred pound cat. "If you want I'll sleep in my truck. I don't like you much after you had that conversation with the brass behind my back. I won't attack you. You don't have to worry about that."

He strode to the door and held it open. Backlit in

the doorframe by the bright sun, he looked like a hulking shadow.

"What I'd worry about if I were you are the bears."

"Bears?"

He let the door shut behind him and didn't turn around to comment further. Molly stood with her eyes closed and took some deep breaths. *I'm sure he's only kidding.*

The smell of him lingered and overcame the faint smell of moldy wood in the cabin. Surrounded by his manly scent, she wanted to feel those strong arms around her and take shelter from always feeling so alone. But he was the wrong man for her. *Primal instinct. Nothing more.*

Bears? Danny? I can do this. But, Kay, I'm going to kill you when I get home.

"Uncle Danneeeeeeee!"

Molly turned toward the door with a smile when she heard the excitement in Mary's voice. She walked outside to the cabin's porch and shaded her eyes with one hand. Sunspots danced as she tried to adjust to the glare. When her field of vision cleared, she stood mute, mouth open.

Amy, not Mary, sprinted into Danny's outstretched arms.

"Missy A!" Danny hollered.

She galloped within two feet of him and then dove forward, both feet off the ground. He caught her with one arm, hoisted her high in the air and spun her, sending her thin legs flying in crazy arcs. Mary tore into the scene and Danny scooped her into the spin with his other arm and whooped, "Missy M!"

Molly's heart ached. Amy hadn't let another man get near her since Eddie's death. How had Danny pulled off this easy playfulness?

He set the girls on their feet and rumpled the

tops of their heads with his knuckles. He looked up at Molly. "Come on, Doctor," he called. "We'll let you play with us."

"Be right there," she answered. "Just want to change into shorts."

She walked into the cabin and secured the door with a slide bolt that half hung off its screws. *A bear could open this door with a sneeze. Do bears sneeze?* She shook her head.

She pulled a pair of shorts from her duffle before she slipped out of her jeans. Her pants were off and on in two motions. She wasn't about to let Dan Sullivan walk in on her in her skivvies.

Outside, she strolled around the grounds ten minutes before she caught sight of Dan and the girls. They stood amid a cluster of other campers on a large wooden deck that fronted a thick stand of trees. Amy and Mary hung on the deck railing on either side of Danny. He looked down the barrel of a rifle that jerked with gunshots into the trees. The metallic chime of a cowbell followed each sharp pop of backfire from the gun.

What the hell is he doing? She ran towards the deck as he handed the gun to Amy and crouched down to help her line up a shot.

"Amy Elizabeth Jordan!" The gun went off and the cowbell's metallic ping sounded. Amy jumped up and down in a victory dance as Molly reached her and ripped the gun out of her hands.

Everyone's stares bored into her. She didn't care what they thought of her. She thrust the gun at Danny and circled Amy with one arm.

"Don't *ever* expose my daughter to guns again." She nudged Amy away with her off the deck.

Danny jogged in front of them. "Molly." He touched her shoulder. "It's only a BB gun."

She shrugged his hand off and walked away.

"Sorry, Molly," he called after her.

74

"Mom," Amy pleaded. "Please don't be mad at me."

"I'm not sweetheart." Molly's constricted throat made it hard for her to speak.

She pushed forward to put as much distance between them and firearms as she could. The thin film of panic sweat on her palms and forehead evaporated with the breeze. As her body cooled the fright dissolved. She squeezed Amy's shoulder as they walked.

She didn't intend to apologize for her reaction. But she did feel the need to explain to her daughter. "I didn't mean to be so stern, honey. But guns terrify me. I don't want you near them."

"Okay, Momma."

They neared a clearing where a group of kids and parents sat at log-hewn picnic tables.

"Let's weave some lanyards," Molly suggested.

****

Planned activities to choose from during the day allowed Molly to have fun with Amy and avoid Danny. But evening approached, and she couldn't avoid the all campers' cookout and marshmallow kabobs around the fire.

As the lake water seemed to drown the sun in a tangerine and plum-colored haze, Molly spied Danny walking toward the campfire.

He wore crisp blue jeans, a torso and biceps hugging black tee shirt and an unbuttoned denim jacket. His long black hair was slicked back from his face, shower damp and curled at the ends.

His eyes searched the group, looking for her. He would try to talk his way out of his earlier misdeed. And he would smell like spicy pine and send out those tractor beams to pull her towards his warmth.

She had already forgiven him for teaching Amy to shoot the BB gun. He couldn't know how she felt about guns, and she didn't blame him. Call it even for talking to his captain behind his back and sentencing him to two weeks of desk duty.

Simple enough to let him off the hook for Amy's shooting lesson, but could she resist the magnetic pull she felt near him? She hoped so. As much as she missed the joy and excitement of intimacy with a man, she wouldn't allow herself to get involved again with one in such a dangerous profession.

His misty green eyes found hers and they locked. She didn't realize she returned his broad smile until he came up to her.

"You're beautiful when you smile," he said. "I hope this means I'm forgiven."

"It does. I abhor guns and the sight of Amy with a gun in her hand, made me a little crazy. You couldn't have known. Am I forgiven for restricting your medical release?"

"I don't have much choice, do I? Besides, my captain doesn't always know what I'm doing. Maybe I'm getting around orders, maybe I'm not." He gave her an enigmatic grin and looked around the campsite. "I better go give a hand at the grills. Want a dog?"

"Sure. Goes great with wine." She held up the bottle.

"Save me a cup."

Molly didn't remember when a hot dog tasted so delicious. Or when she felt this light and free. Tucked in the woods, far away from the ambulance bay, she could relax and enjoy her child, the pungent smell of the bonfire, and paper cup toasts to the sales success of the Charity Girls.

Despite her resolve not to get entangled with Dan, she was flattered when he settled next to her by the fire. He draped his jacket around her shoulders when the evening air chilled.

They roasted marshmallows on sticks and licked molten candy goo off their fingers and lips. She liked the way Amy and Mary gravitated towards Dan.

He handled skewering the marshmallows on pointy sticks and doled out the treats to each girl. Then he hung over them with discreet vigilance so neither of them drew too close to the blazing fire. He talked to them without a trace of condescension and seemed genuine about wanting them near him.

Molly felt less confident about his nearness to her when the kids, and some of the parents, decided to head to the cabins and call it a day.

She got up and dusted off the seat of her jeans with both hands. "About those sleeping arrangements?" She looked up into his eyes and saw reflected firelight dance there.

"Come walk with me." He held out his hand.

"I think I'll get some rest."

She held out her hand toward him as if she were dreaming. Logic told her to say good night and walk away. But she remained, lost in his eyes and the memory of a fantasy. She placed her hand in his and felt instant comfort when he closed his fingers around it. She let him draw her forward and walked by his side.

He led her under an arch of tree branches along a mulch-covered path that skirted the lake perimeter. She heard muted crackles and spark pops from the campfire. The only other sounds were their foot-scuffs on the forest bed and her accelerated heartbeat.

"Beautiful," he said.

His voice seemed magnified amid the hushed, velvet gray that surrounded them. Through the thin trees on the banks of the lake, mirrored moonlight shimmered.

"It is a beautiful night," she whispered.

"I didn't mean the night."

She turned into his kiss without thinking. Her lips met his and touched, softly poised on the edge of where she shouldn't go. His hand cupped the back of her neck and his fingers laced up into her hair. They deepened the kiss with equal hunger. She molded her body against his, thrilled by the fit, the feel of him and the melt of desire that dissolved her restraint.

He didn't hurry the kiss or move his hands to caress her. They hung, suspended in that perfect connection in the silent forest, until his lips released hers as gently as the kiss began. When she opened her eyes and looked up at him, he smiled.

"Thank you," he said.

He held her in his arms; the only reason she still stood upright. "You're welcome," was all she could think to say.

When her legs felt like flesh and bone again, she disconnected from him. He resumed walking deeper into the forest at an unhurried pace and she walked along with him. Her emotions warred within her, equal measures of fear and ecstasy. She was afraid to go too far with Danny and ecstatic to know that he wanted her as she wanted him.

The path looped around and soon Molly saw the outlines of the picnic grove and the glow of the dying campfire through the trees. Her lips tingled in memory of his kiss. She tasted him on her tongue and felt the massage of his hand on her neck.

Alive with desire, she was close to abandoning the "hands off the policeman" motto she lived. But she didn't know what to say to him, or what to do next. She hiked with him up the lawn to their cabin. The incline of the hill pulled at the backs of her calves and upped her heart rate even more than he already had.

When they reached the cabin, he pushed the door open ahead of her and turned back to face her. He made a "shush" and a "stay-here" gesture with one hand. He went inside and came out with a sleeping bag rolled under his arm.

"I'll go bunk in my truck," he assured her.

"Danny, that isn't necessary," she whispered. "I'll feel terrible knowing you're uncomfortable. You can stay in the cabin. I trust you."

His face in shadows, she could still make out the bloom of dimples on his cheeks as he smiled down at her. "I don't."

He jumped down the two wooden steps in one bound and headed towards the parking area.

"Danny!"

"Yes, Doc."

"What about bears?"

"No problem." He patted his hip. "I'm packing."

His laughter receded as he walked away from her. She stood on the porch and debated going after him. She didn't. In a few seconds her head controlled her heart.

Before sunlight she carried her sleeping child to their car and left.

Chapter 10

Dan sat at his dilapidated desk and wadded paper into balls. He launched them the eight or so feet across his office toward a wire wastepaper basket, hitting more than he missed.

He stopped his impromptu game and stared at the evidence board he had set up next to his desk. Oblivious to the noise in the squad room outside his door, he struggled to profile the HH Killer and break the case. He was missing something. His instincts told him that it was right there in front of him, but it remained out of reach and ran circles in his mind.

His head throbbed with the frustration of not being able to grasp the missing puzzle piece. Redheads. Redheads. It didn't help that a woman with a glowing cap of platinum hair kept getting in the way.

He had to stop his mind from wandering to how halos glowed around Molly Jordan's moonlight colored hair in the Wisconsin woods. She seeped into his mind too often during the day. The heat from their kiss lingered. He tasted her on his lips and felt her body mold to his. It made him hungry to wrap her in his arms and taste more of her. He was falling hard for her and he didn't like the feeling. He had a killer to catch. He could not let himself be distracted.

No one had ever taken his mind off a case. Why now? What was there about Dr. Jordan that had his palms sweating like a schoolboy? She even haunted his dreams.

He was thankful when Joe rapped on the door jam.

"Hey Danny."

"Hey. Nice face. You look like a jaundiced raccoon. I'd like to see the other guy. Oh, wait. I mean the other girl."

"Funny. As if I haven't taken enough crap over this. It does get old, you know."

"Not for me."

"I can always count on my brother." Joe shook his head and inspected Danny's woefully cluttered office. Files piled on the desk and lined the scuffed, linoleum floor behind it in uneven heaps. Wadded balls of trash dotted a trail to the wastebasket.

"How do you find anything in this mess?"

"Don't even think about touching anything again."

"Not in a million years."

"I'm still trying to figure out where you put things after you decided to be Mom for a day."

"You were a raging pain in my ass over the whole thing. And I thought I did you a favor. Last time I'll do that. I still don't know how you work like this. Let's just agree to disagree on workspaces."

A young, tall cop bent his head under the doorframe and poked it into Dan's office. At six ten he was the pride of the department's basketball team. "Hey Lieutenant. Hey Joe. Me and the guys are heading out now for the gym to warm up before the game."

"As if you need to warm up, Nick," Danny quipped. "We're right behind you."

Dan stood and looked at the evidence board one last time before covering it for the night. "Damn it, Joe. What is it that I am missing? We have to stop this asshole before he kills again. Three murders in a couple months and I have nothing."

"Stop beating yourself up about this. You're not the only one working on the case. We'll catch him. He'll slip up and we'll get him. It's just a matter of time."

"We don't have time." Dan pulled the cloth he rigged to cover the evidence board. "I keep saying him."

"Yeah, so?" Joe grabbed an end of the cloth and tucked it over a corner of the board.

"Could be a woman. It's a stretch and she'd have to be strong, but it's possible. There's no sexual violence. The slashes across the eyes, the intent to blind the victims—could add up to a lot of things. Maybe the slashes are supposed to be crosses. Might be religious."

Danny shrugged into his leather bomber jacket and slung his Nike gym bag over his shoulder. "Let's check out the victims' religions. Maybe there's a connection I've been missing."

"Okay. I'll get right on it," Joe said.

"No. I think I'm chasing air with this, too. Tomorrow's soon enough. Let's go kick some fireman ass."

"That's what I came to talk to you about. I can't play tonight."

Dan stopped short with his hand poised over the light switch. "You're kidding me, right? We don't have a chance of beating the firemen without our All-American point guard."

"Well, Dr. Jordan said..."

Dan outstretched an angled palm and silenced Joe.

"Don't tell me. Dr. Jordan said that you couldn't

play with a broken nose. Just like she told the Captain I couldn't go back to work and stuck me behind a desk for two weeks when I should have been out in the field working the case. Two weeks lost. I can't believe that you are going to let a little broken nose keep you off the court."

"She said I should avoid contact sports for a few weeks. The firemen match gets pretty rough."

"Do what you want tonight. Sit with the wives and girlfriends and catch up on the gossip. I don't care."

Dan switched off the light and stormed out of his office. The cops at their desks did not look up as he passed. Voices traveled in the close quarters of the squad room and Dan hadn't been quiet. Anyone who had been on duty had experienced Dan's fury for the two weeks he was chained to the desk. Bent heads meant staying off the end of Dan's anger tonight.

He knew he was being unreasonable, but Molly's interference seemed to affect every part of his life lately — even a little competitive recreation. It was unfair to take out his frustrations on his brother, but he figured Joe would get over it.

He let the door slam behind him and stalked through the parking lot to his car. Before he had a chance to pull out of his reserved spot, Joe tapped on the window. Dan rolled it down.

"What?"

"Can I catch a ride to the gym?"

"Get in."

"I'm playing."

"Look, Joe. I'm sorry. I was out of line back there. I'm just frustrated with the case. I'm pissed at Molly for sidelining me. I'm angry in general lately. Don't let my bad mood make you do something you don't want to do. Maybe she's right and you shouldn't play tonight."

"I'm playing."

"You sure?"

Joe nodded.

"Okay, then. Let's show those firemen what the Sullivan boys can do."

****

The policemen were down by one point with ten seconds left on the play clock. The firemen smelled victory. Joe had sunk a fair share of shots, but he had been off his game all night.

Dan threw the ball in bounds to Nick, who dribbled, then shot it back to Dan. Nick streaked to the basket pulling the firemen with him.

Dan glanced at Joe. He was sweating and his bruised eyes seemed darker against his pale skin. Dan's arm throbbed like a bitch. Win or lose in the next eight seconds and then they could relax over a blessed beer and some pizza.

Five seconds remained, and Joe knew it was coming. Dan faked the throw to Nick and passed the ball behind his back to Joe who launched a perfect arc. The ball swished through the hoop as the buzzer sounded. The brothers had practiced that exact shot in the driveway for hours.

Cheers erupted as the policemen finally beat their rivals. After doling out back slaps, good-natured ribs and running the gauntlet shaking the hands of the opposition, Dan put his arm around Joe's shoulders. They headed towards the locker room.

"My arm is killing me." Dan rotated his right shoulder and flexed his arm a few times.

"My nose feels like a catcher's mitt on my face. I can't breathe."

"Great time, wasn't it?"

Joe grinned. "Sure was."

Chapter 11

Molly couldn't face going home to an empty house after the emotional day she had at work. Amy was at a sleepover and Bobbie had a class. Even though she knew Bobbie would have left something for her to warm for dinner, when she was finally able to leave the hospital she decided to go out to dinner instead.

She pulled into a prime parking space that opened just as she turned the corner into the quaint center of downtown Naperville. She parked only a few feet away from the restaurant, a piece of luck she didn't expect the way the day had gone so far.

She braced herself for the bitter November wind that launched leaves along the sidewalk in swirling flocks, pulled up her coat collar and jogged into the converted firehouse turned Lou Malnati's Restaurant. That time of year in the Chicago environs made you forget that you were ever warm.

The homey feel of her favorite eatery enveloped her. She inhaled the mixed buttery and spicy scents of Italian cooking: oregano, onions, garlic, basil and tomato. Her stomach growled anticipating comfort food and pizza that was worth every single calorie.

Her lucky timing held and she was able to grab a booth in the back of the establishment across from the party room. She knew it really wasn't luck, but Dawn's special magic. Molly met the restaurant manager when her little boy was rushed into the emergency room with an allergic reaction to a bee sting. Dawn would never forget the caring way Molly had interacted with her son. Dawn left word with her staff that Molly should be treated like a queen whenever she came into the restaurant.

An efficient waitress took her drink order, and soon she sipped her diet coke. Cabernet would be better, but off-limits since she had to drive home. She browsed the menu despite knowing she would order her usual meal. She read the list of items anyway and tried but didn't succeed to forget the events of her workday.

A drunk driver had altered a family's life forever. Molly's team tried to save a mother and her two little boys. Despite all their cumulative knowledge, they couldn't.

Mike Lynch and his surgical team pulled the daughter through. The husband, although still in poor condition, would recover, also.

It was a miracle that anyone in the family's car survived. But the horror on the father's face and his moans of agony when he was told about his catastrophic loss haunted Molly. She could empathize with his reaction to the tragedy of losing a spouse. She couldn't imagine the utter devastation that would result from the loss of two children at the same time.

She never got used to losing a patient. Despite the abject misery she felt every time it happened, she hoped she never would. The irony was, the drunk only suffered bruises and was able to walk on his own power when the police handcuffed him and led him out of her emergency room.

She shut her eyes and willed herself to stop thinking about things she couldn't change and to relax. She was thankful that Amy and Bobbie weren't waiting for her at home. Sometimes she just needed a break from people's dependence on her.

A loud burst of laugher erupted from the party room and drew her attention. Life went on. People around her were enjoying themselves and having a great time. It made her feel isolated, but better.

She spotted Dawn and waved.

Dawn changed direction and headed over to Molly's booth.

"Dr. Jordan, it's great to see you. Is Amy in the arcade room?"

"No, I'm by myself tonight. I had a little free time and just wanted to get out and be with people."

"Tough day, huh?"

"Yes. I'm trying to regroup."

Molly handed Dawn the menu. "I don't know why I even look at this." She smiled up at her. "I always order the same thing. I'm just too predictable."

"Cheese cubes, Lou Malnati's salad, and a deep dish sausage pizza. Large to take home leftovers."

"Yes. I'm definitely too predictable."

"Let me put in your order and I'll bring out your appetizer."

Molly leaned into the vinyl backrest of the booth, sipped more soda and people-watched. Her tension eased as she observed the happy families around her.

A few men went into the party room, and the laughter, presumably fueled by the pitchers of beer she noticed being brought into the room earlier, boomed.

Dawn returned with the cheese cubes.

"They're on the house."

"You spoil me."

"I like to take care of my special regulars."

"What's up in the party room tonight? They're getting louder and louder."

"A bunch of our regulars. They come in every Friday night during basketball season. They have a league. Tonight they're celebrating the victory of the policemen over the firemen in a charity game. They play the game every year and usually the firemen win. In fact, I can't remember the last time the policemen won. I was sorry I had to work tonight. I go to the game every year."

Dawn slid into the booth, opposite Molly, and leaned forward conspiringly. "Mmmm, all those lean, buff bodies sweating and running up and down the court," she said in a low voice.

On cue an overweight man left the party room, and turned toward the men's room in the back of the restaurant. He was bald, about fifty years old and his shirt buttons strained against the huge belly that bulged over his belt.

Molly and Dawn exchanged glances and burst out laughing.

"I guess I didn't miss anything stuck at work tonight, after all." Dawn stood up and wiped tears from the corners of her eyes.

The party room doorway filled with the lean, buff body Dawn had described, his head turned back into the room away from them. Molly recognized Dan. She didn't see his face, but she couldn't mistake that body or the sound of his hearty laughter. The sight of him set off a flash of adrenaline through her that blazed heat to her cheeks and made her heart somersault.

"Now, that's more like it." Dawn said, looking in Dan's direction. "Whew, is it me, or did the temperature just go up a few degrees?" She walked away, openly gazing at Dan's physique.

Molly let out a shaky breath and straightened

her spine against the padded booth. Dan turned out of the room. Their eyes met.

All the ambient noise in the restaurant stopped. Molly's heart pounded so loudly that the people in the next booth must have heard it, too. *Calm down, Molly. You can't want him.*

She couldn't break his stare. She didn't listen to her inner voice. She envisioned a kiss in the moonlight while gentle lake waters lapped against the shore.

He took his time walking over to her table, which didn't help her pulse rate. He sat down on the opposite side of her booth. She smelled musky sweat mixed with his aftershave and heat rose in her chest with an elevator fall of desire deep in her belly.

"What an unexpected surprise. How are you, Molly?" His voice was pleasant, but he didn't smile.

"I'm fine and you?"

"Good. Thanks. Yeah, I'm good. You meeting someone?"

"No. I'm here alone."

"We need to talk. We have some unfinished business."

She couldn't let one napalm kiss make her forget all that she worked so hard to protect. "No, I think we finished everything."

"No, we didn't."

"Well, I disagree."

"You always disagree." He stared at her. "Except once. I know you felt what I felt. I know you wanted to kiss me. I know you want to kiss me again."

"I had a rough day today, Dan. I'm not up to sparring with you." She sighed and wished she were home in bed. She wouldn't give in to the temptation to invite Dan to join her there.

"Where did you go on Sunday? I was up before daybreak, and you were already gone."

He looked disappointed.

"Um...I had to get back. I didn't want to disturb you," she stammered, knowing she was a coward.

"You disturb me all the time." He grinned and reached for Molly's hand. "I want you to disturb me."

She pulled her hand away on reflex. "Well..." She tugged on the ends of her hair. "It's not always about what you want."

He shoved his hands into the pockets of his sweatpants and slouched back in the booth. "I don't want to fight with you. Want to join our victory party?"

She smiled at him as rowdy laugher exploded from the party room and somebody started up a chorus of "O Danny Boy."

"Apparently you're being paged."

He smiled and nodded.

"You better get back to your friends."

He stood up so abruptly that he bumped into the waitress who balanced a large, pizza pan and salad bowl in each hand.

"Sorry." He helped her set them on Molly's table. "You must be hungry, Doc. Want me to help you eat all this?"

"No, thanks. I'm fine. Have a good time at your party. Congratulations for winning the charity game."

"Yeah, thanks." He clenched his jaw, his face looked frozen and all his body language pointed away from Molly. "Sorry I bothered you. See you around."

She watched him walk away. He didn't turn back before he disappeared into the private room.

Damn him. I don't want to feel this way.

She wanted what she refused to have—a man who courted death every day. Her history haunted her. Better not to let this get beyond a bone-vaporizing kiss. *Okay, brain. Notify my heart.*

"Hey, Mol. Mind if I sit down?"

Mike Lynch stood where Dan stood minutes before, poised to sit at her table.

"Of course. Sit down. Aren't you working tonight?"

"It's my night to pick up the pizzas for the floor."

"Wow, that's service for your staff. Most of the doctors just order a delivery."

"I've had pizza delivered, too, but Malnati's doesn't go as far as the hospital and I was in the mood for pan pizza. Plus I have a very pregnant wife who told me I was in the mood for pan pizza and to drop some off for her on the my way back."

He smiled, picked off an edge of crust from Molly's pizza and ate it. His smile vanished. "Wish I could order a stiff drink. Can't get that father's face out of my mind."

"Same with me. That's why I came here. I needed the distraction. The girls are out tonight and I just didn't want to be alone."

"Don't let me interrupt your dinner."

"You're not. Would you like some salad while you wait?"

"You don't have to ask me twice."

She piled a plate with fresh greens, Fontina cheese, diced tomatoes, and salami pieces; passed it to him and then helped herself to a smaller portion. She rested her hand on top of his and smiled.

"Thanks for stopping at my table. I needed a friendly face tonight."

"No problem and thanks for the salad. I'm starving." He dug in.

After he cleaned his plate, he slumped back in the seat and rubbed his flat stomach. "Whew. That filled some of the hole."

Dawn walked past their table and let Mike know his order was ready at the front counter.

"I hate to eat and run, but there are a few nurses who will have my head if I don't get back soon with dinner. And Kay? She'll have more than my head. Feeling any better?"

"I am. Thanks."

"No problem."

She watched Mike work his way around the wooden tables and chairs. She signaled the waitress with a wave and asked her to box up the untouched pizza. Bobbie and Amy would enjoy it tomorrow. She had no appetite for it. She paid the bill, bundled up, grasped her Styrofoam take-out boxes and shivered her way to her car.

All she wanted was to be home, away from being a spectator of other people's fun and the lure of the man in the party room.

****

Molly didn't notice him stewing in the doorway. Blood surged in the veins of Dan's neck. He clenched and unclenched his fists. He knew she wouldn't be able to eat all that food herself. When Mike showed up, it all fell into place. She refused to be with a cop but had no problem messing around with the big-shot surgeon. The *married* big-shot surgeon. The hypocrite. He should have known. Women are all alike. And what was Mike thinking?

When he had called Mike to ask him to the game, he said he had to work. It was convenient that his mistress worked with him. Look at the timing. She brushed him off minutes before meeting her lover and following him out with their after-sex pizza picnic.

She'd looked nervous when he talked with her earlier. He chalked that up to the effect he thought he had on her. He resented the effect she had on him. He shook his head and felt a surge of disgust. Good thing he hadn't gotten tangled up with the seductress. All that innocent, blushing crap was pure bullshit.

He needed to cool down before he confronted

them. They weren't getting away with this. He had his sister and her children to think of. He rolled his shoulders, plastered on a smile and turned back to his teammates.

Chapter 12

The early morning telephone call didn't wake Danny. He hadn't slept all night. He spent eight hours staring at the ceiling and mulling over his brother-in-law's infidelity. He tried to decide how best to tell Kay, considering her delicate condition. The tangled sheets around his legs were proof that his restless deliberations hadn't yielded a plan to break the news to her.

He picked up the phone on the second ring and answered it with a clipped, "Yeah."

"Hi, Uncle Danny. It's me, Mikey. Mom just put four pumpkin breads in the oven."

Dan smiled at his nephew's whispered announcement. "Thanks, little man. I owe you."

He heard only a click in response and laughed heartily. His enterprising nephew would call another uncle with the promise of baked goods fresh from Kay's oven.

The uncles would never rat out their nephew. Each was more than willing to fork over five bucks to him for Kay's baked goods. Her homemade, meatball lasagna was well worth the ten dollars that Mikey charged for that heads-up phone call.

The phone call was just the push Dan needed to give up his attempt to sleep or solve the problem of the Lou Malnati's tryst that he had witnessed last evening. A hot shower would clear his head so he could figure out how to approach his sister. First, he'd out Mike to Kay. Then he'd visit Mike's office and confront him head on. Maybe he'd hit the trifecta with an unannounced visit to Molly Jordan's office, too.

The thought of Molly made his chest constrict. He wasn't accustomed to those feelings in recent memory and didn't want to label them. No woman could spin him around like that after just one kiss. He refused to consider that he might be jealous. He didn't care what Molly did, he told himself. He had to protect his sister.

****

Kay leaned her thigh against the large, picnic-style table in her cheery kitchen with her arms rested on the shelf under her breasts provided by her protruding belly. She had no sooner taken the pumpkin breads out of the oven and placed them on the racks to cool, when she heard the back door open.

Joe walked into her kitchen, followed a few minutes later by Patrick, then Dan, and she heard Brian's truck pull into the driveway.

"How do you guys know when I'm baking? Can you smell it or what? This is freaking mystifying." She watched each sibling straddle the bench seat and tuck long legs under her table. They made themselves at home and devoured the bread.

Brian walked through the back door.

"Aren't you happy to see me?" He kissed her on the top of the head and nudged Patrick out of the way to get a seat closer to the food. "Can't I just come over to see my favorite sister?"

"Favorite sister, huh? Very funny. I'll start the

tea." She walked to the commercial gas stove and lifted a red enameled teakettle off one grate.

"No, Sis. Sit." Dan got up and took the kettle out of her hand. "I'll get the tea. You rest."

Laughter and conversation filled the room. Kay sat down with the men and indulged in a slice of bread while she doled out and withstood sibling verbal jabs laced with sarcasm. When the last piece of bread was fought over and won, the men drifted off to start their day.

****

Dan hung behind, cleared the table and loaded mugs and plates into the dishwasher.

Kay sat and watched him work. "You're quiet today, Dan. And I usually have to beg you to even put a mug in the sink no less load the dishwasher. What's up?"

He kept his back to her and gazed out the window over the sink that was framed by yellow gingham curtains that she made herself. It enraged him more to think of her making a happy home for her cheating husband. "I have to ask you something and I don't want to hurt you or upset you."

"What? Go ahead and ask."

Her voice sounded wary and it made him feel worse for what he was about to do. He turned toward her. The innocent expression on her face almost undid him. "Where was Mike last night?"

"Mike? This is about Mike? He was at the hospital. Where else would he be? And you know he was there. Didn't you call and invite him to the game last night? I remember he was disappointed that he had to work and miss the charity game."

"What if I told you he lied to us and he wasn't at work?"

"Mike doesn't lie."

He grabbed a dishtowel and dried his hands with it as he walked to where she sat. "Are you sure of that?" He sat at the table across from her.

"Enough. What are you trying to tell me? Just say it."

She stiffened to withstand whatever he told her. "I saw Mike having dinner last night with someone," he said.

"Where? With whom?"

"He was at Malnati's. You know the guys always go there after a game."

"I do know that. And Mike knows I know that. Who was with him?"

"Dr. Jordan"

"Molly Jordan?"

"I'm sorry to be the one to tell you. But I thought you would want to know."

She didn't crumble like he had feared. She looked surprisingly calm.

"You saw them having dinner together and you didn't go over to them and say something?" she asked.

"I was going to, but they left before I had a chance to confront them."

"You saw them leave together?"

"Not exactly."

"But you're sure they left together."

"Well, not exactly."

"I wonder."

"What?"

"I wonder if Mike had Molly hiding in his car when he stopped here to drop off the pizza that I craved so badly last night that I badgered him to get some for me. I wonder if Molly went to the hospital with him to drop off the other six pizzas he had in the car for the staff, since it was his night to supply the food. I wonder if you have a brain in that thick skull of yours." She folded her hands, rested them on the table in front of her and stared at him with unblinking, gray-blue eyes.

"She might have followed him in her car. Or maybe they sneak around at the hospital. They were holding hands."

"Holding hands? You're sure you saw that?" she fired at him.

"Yeah." He scratched his head and the indignation he wrestled with all night faded. "Maybe it was more like she put her hand over his hand."

"Wow, that's an indictment if I ever heard one. Any woman who touches a man *must* be sleeping with him."

Kay picked up the dishtowel and threw it at Dan's head. It landed, flattened and draped his face with a cockeyed veil.

"You're ridiculous," she said dismissively and shot him a look of superiority.

He took the towel off his head and laid it on the table. "It's just that…"

Kay gave him her famous get-to-the-truth of the matter glare. "Molly's due here soon. Today is crafts day for Mary's Charity Girls troop and we're going to make Thanksgiving cornucopias. I'm their leader so they're all coming here. She called last night to confirm the time. She called from her home. I was just taking my first bite of pizza. I can show you the caller ID record on the phone if you want, Detective."

"Jesus. I'm sorry, Kay. I shouldn't have said anything. Forgive me?"

"There's nothing to forgive. Trust me. I would want you to tell me if Mike were stupid enough to try something that crazy. I might be retired, but I've kept up my shooting skills and he knows it.

"Want to stick around and help us with the crafting project?"

"No way." He jumped up, sauntered to the door and stopped, hand resting on the doorknob. "Please don't say anything to Mike or Molly about this, okay?"

She looked at him with the truth-ferreting expression she inherited from their mother. "Is there something going on between you and Molly?"

"Nope."

He saw her register the truth in her eyes as she walked over and faced him. "But you want something to be going on between you."

"Even if I did, which I am not saying I do, she wants no part of a cop."

He kissed her cheek and swung out the door before she could respond. He felt guilty for his stupidity. But he was wrong about Molly and that gave his spirits a huge lift.

****

Molly woke up and dressed early so she could whip up a coffee cake to bring to Kay's. She looked forward to spending time with the Charity Girls. Well, maybe not all of them, especially making cornucopias. But, she did want to be with Amy and looked forward to spending time with Kay.

She left a note for Bobbie, who enjoyed the treat of sleeping in and carried the warm coffee cake to her car feeling capable and domestic.

She missed getting together with other mothers since she moved to Chicago. She hoped to grow closer to Kay. They had so much in common. Amy and Mary acted like sisters. She enjoyed working with Mike. They both cared a great deal for Dan...

Now where did that come from?

She blanked thoughts of the man from her mind as she cleared security in the exclusive gated community and arrived at the stately Lynch home. The burnt sienna brick house with a columned portico reminded her of the ante-bellum mansions in the Deep South. An expansive carpet of thick green grass stretched in front of the house like a Kentucky meadow. A wide, paved-brick driveway snaked in a "U" from two aprons off the street on either side of the property. Skateboards, bikes, a tricycle and several balls littered the driveway and fringes of the lawn.

The massive, wood-carved front door flew open before she had the keys out of the ignition. Amy hopped over to the car, Mary close behind.

"Hi, Ma. What took you so long? We've been waiting forever for you to come."

Amy put her thin arms around Molly's waist and leaned toward the foiled-wrapped package in her mother's hands. "Is that coffee cake I smell?"

"Yep. I made it this morning."

"It smells great, Mrs. Jordan," Mary said. "My mom is in the kitchen. She said to go on in."

"Okay."

Amy beamed up at her. "Mrs. Lynch put us in charge of all the supplies for crafts day. We're setting everything up in the den. Wait until you see all the plastic fruits Mary and I picked out last night at the Dollar Store. This is going to be the best project yet."

The girls pulled Molly into the house and hurried back to their assigned task.

She followed the sound of a whistling teakettle and found her way to the kitchen. Kay stood on a stepladder and reached for something on the top of the refrigerator.

"Whoa, Kay. What are you doing? Let me get whatever you're reaching for up there."

"I almost have it. Gotcha." Kay tugged an aluminum foil bundle out from behind a white wicker basket. "It's getting harder and harder to find hiding places." She descended the ladder, careful with the placement of each foot on the steps.

Molly put the coffee cake on the table, leery that Kay would fall with one hand holding a package, and hurried to help her.

Safe on the ground, Kay inhaled deeply. "Is that

cinnamon I smell?"

"It is. And lots of butter, too. I made a coffee cake this morning. We can have a piece before the troop gets here."

"One coffee cake?"

"Well, yes. Should I have made more than one?" Molly hoped she hadn't made a social gaffe.

"No. No. I was just wondering out loud what it might be like to make one coffee cake, just one cake. And actually have it last long enough to cool. Please sit down. What kind of hostess am I?"

She opened the foil package and placed it next to Molly's coffee cake.

"That looks delicious. What is it?"

"That's all that's left of four, good-sized, pumpkin breads I made this morning. When they weren't looking I cut two pieces and hid them so we would have them."

"Who are they?"

"My brothers. I don't know how they know. But every time, no lie, every time I bake anything, they show up. Anyway. At least I salvaged something for us. Let's just enjoy our peace, quiet and tea before the other girls get here. This cake looks delicious. Thanks for making it. You'll have to give me your recipe."

Kay cut two thick slices.

"Sure. Thanks for inviting me over. I've been looking forward to this all week."

"Well, we shall see if you still want to thank me after a few hours of craft projects with the Charity Girls." Kay laughed.

Molly had just taken a mouthful of tea when Kay casually asked, "So, Molly, how long have you been having an affair with my husband?"

Tea shot out of Molly's nose. She gagged and sputtered.

Kay jumped up and patted Molly on the back.

"Gee, that didn't go as planned. I thought you'd laugh."

"Excuse me?" Molly gasped for breath.

Kay plunked down on her seat. "I'm sorry. I thought you would think it was funny."

"Funny? What could possibly be funny about my having an affair with Mike?"

"Dan was here this morning."

"Dan?"

"He was at Malnati's last night."

"I know. I saw him and talked to him."

"Mike was there, too."

"I know. I saw Mike and talked to him, also. I'm lost here, Kay."

"Dan saw you and Mike together. For some reason he put two and two together and got five."

"Let me get this straight. Your brother told you I'm having an affair with Mike?"

"In so many words."

"Your brother is a jackass."

"Well, that goes without saying."

"I am *not* having an affair with your husband. I respect and admire him and I would never... What kind of woman do you think I am?"

"I never thought for one minute that you had designs on my husband. You wouldn't be sitting at my table if I had the slightest doubt. I thought it was interesting when Dan told me. In fact I thought Dan must be interested in you."

"Your brother is just mad because I don't fall drooling at his feet like other women."

"He did ask me not to tell you."

"Well, of course he did. Why would he want his family to contribute to my low opinion of him? Thanks for telling me. I'll handle your brother," she promised.

"I'd like to be a fly on the wall when you... handle Dan." Kay flashed her a sly smile. "So you have a low opinion of him, huh?"

The doorbell interrupted any further discussion.

Three hours passed as Molly fumbled around and followed Kay's expert instructions to make Thanksgiving centerpieces.

"You would think that if I can wield a scalpel, I can use a simple glue gun," she told Kay.

She was sticky with glue and the fruit on her cornucopia kept falling off. But she had fun in the warmth of Kay's patience and the flowering of a new friendship.

When she finished playing Martha Stewart, she thought about how to handle Dan.

Chapter 13

Molly had stewed the last few days over Dan's ridiculous notion that she was the other woman in Mike's life. It riled her more when she heard Danny's casual tone on the telephone. He said that he just wanted to drop off the jacket that Amy had left in his car. And she had told him, just as casually, that it was convenient for him to drop by.

Kay probably hadn't told him that she knew about his false accusations. *Good. All the better to hammer him for the idiot that he is. Conceited ass.*

Glad she was alone to confront him, she heard a car engine shut off outside her door. She didn't want Amy or Bobbie to overhear anything about the embarrassing situation. The doorbell chimed and she walked, unhurried, to answer it.

She wore snug jeans, a fitted, waistband-skimming sweater of powder blue cashmere and matching socks. She thought the color brought out the fire in her eyes. She stopped to fluff her hair in the hall mirror and checked her lipstick. She rationalized that her touch of vanity that day boosted her confidence to gain the upper hand with Dan.

She opened the door and waved him in, mute and unsmiling. He seemed unfazed by the silent treatment.

"Hey, Molly. You look beautiful today. Here's the jacket." He handed it to her.

She took it, turned away and hung it in the hall closet. She spun around, faced him and fired, "You are a conceited ass, Daniel Sullivan. I'm going to have my say and then I want you to leave my house."

His smile dimmed and his green eyes darkened like a tornado sky. "Wait just a minute—"

"No, you wait a minute." She poked a finger in his chest. It felt like she poked a wall. "I cannot believe that your ego is so huge that you can appoint yourself judge and jury of my morals. You will not tell lies behind my back..."

He stepped toward her and pushed her finger back with his chest. Only the distance of her bent elbow separated them.

"Lady, do you ever have a conversation that doesn't involve shooting orders at people?"

"This isn't a conversation." She stared into his angry eyes with equal force. "This is I talk, you listen. How dare you tell Mike's wife that I'm his mistress?"

"Kay isn't Mike's wife, she's *my* sister..." He circled her hand in his palm and pulled her finger away from him.

She yanked her hand away and paced. "Just because I didn't want to have dinner with you, doesn't give you the right to fabricate motives of...of...adultery!" She was breathless, her voice just short of shrill.

"Christ, you'd think I hung a scarlet letter around your neck and marched you to the stockade, Hester," he derided.

Her eyebrows shot up.

"What? You think a dumb cop hasn't read literature here and there?" He moved toward her and her heart skittered.

"Don't." She mustered as much authority as she could to spit out the command.

"Don't what?" He advanced, looming over her. His eyes bored into hers. She refused to break the stare or back away.

He stopped, inches away from her. He stood there, too near, muscles tensed, poised on the edge of her danger zone. Their chests heaved with ragged breaths. She read the dare in his eyes.

All she held back from him, all the denial of what she wanted with him no longer made sense to her. The self-imposed constraints fell away like handcuffs clattering to the floor. She moved toward him at the same time he moved toward her.

Their bodies fused as their lips crushed together. They fed on lips and tongue and interlaced breath. Tiny moans echoed in the expansive hallway. His hands slid up and down her spine, over and under the soft folds of cashmere. Her skin flamed, branded where he touched and prickled with goose bumps where his hand passed over to ignite another spot.

She twined her tongue with his and threaded her fingers in the soft, thick hair that curled around the nape of his neck. He turned her in his embrace, circled his hand around her waist and slid it up under her sweater to engulf her breast in his palm. She sucked in her breath and thrilled at his throaty groan when his fingers furrowed under lace and dove to caress her naked flesh.

Her breath caught as her nipple tightened, her body swelled with desire and her legs trembled. She swayed within the arc of his strong arm, helpless to stop him from doing anything he wanted with her. With her eyes closed, she saw dark shadows cover her eyelids as he skimmed the sweater over her head. His arms lifted her high off the floor and swept her higher as he climbed the stairs.

Her arms circled his neck and she smiled into his shoulder, her lips brushing the new scar there.

"No, Rhett," she whispered. "My bedroom's back down on the first floor, through the French doors."

He reversed and swung her legs over the railing as he bounded down and turned into her room. They tumbled together on her bed, grasping, rolling, their lips melded. Her hands coursed over his body so differently than the clinical examination the first time she touched the hard planes and ridges. Now she meant to give pleasure, to drive him as wild as he drove her. She wanted him skin to skin.

"Let me." He brushed her hands away from the button of her jeans, peeled them off and flung them to the floor. His hands grasped her hips and pulled her upwards, his hot breath scorching the tender flesh beneath her flimsy, silk panties.

He tugged away the material and covered her with his mouth, fingers kneading. Her hips bucked and pressed into his searing exploration. A current of need charged through her. Her hunger for him overwhelmed her and she thought it would destroy her if she didn't feed until he filled her.

Her hands wove into his hair as she stiffened with the piercing burst inside her. White light blazed in front of her eyelids. She had no chance to recover before he threw off his shirt, rolled, and angled her astride him. A quick twist unhooked her bra. He pulled it away, tossed it over the side of the bed and brought his face up between her breasts.

"Electric silk," he whispered, his voice thick and sultry.

Her lips found his and she delighted in how he responded to first the soft, then the searching pressures she used to arouse him. She lined a path of kisses on his neck, down his torso, over the silken hair of his chest.

Drunk with pleasure, she thrilled at the velvet, etched bands of muscle and his absolute surrender of control to her. His arms rested at his sides and he let her have her way.

She stripped off the rest of his clothes and pressed her body over his, every nerve ending alive and quaking. He rolled them again, and she gasped as he entered her and filled her.

"I want you," he breathed in her hair.

"I want you," she answered, exulting in the perfect fit of their bodies, the shining place where Dan took her.

They rocked and pitched, clung to each other, and gasped as their passion mounted. They ascended in a dizzy rush and cried out as they reached the crest together.

They lay spent, their bodies still fused. His weight pressed her deep into the mattress and the part of her he had sent soaring came back to rest in her body. Crushed, she withstood it as a kind of punishment for making love with him. She wanted the weight of the moment to be literal as well as figurative.

So many thoughts flew around her head. She imagined that Eddie watched her with Dan. Wondering if he would think her unfaithful caused a stab of pain. If he could somehow see her could he also read her mind? Did he know that she felt free and wondrously alive for the first time since his death? He would know that she wouldn't give her body unless she cared for a man. Did he feel her begin to care for someone else besides him?

"I'm crushing you," Dan said. He shifted off her and propped on his elbows at her side.

She turned toward him and searched his eyes as if they held her answers. He brushed the back of his hand across her cheek, closed his eyes for a second and looked at her again. His smile teased his dimples, and then he smiled with his whole face. His eyes gleamed with emotion. Perhaps she did find her answers there.

She looked up at him and conscience pangs gave way to a sense of peace. She could have a healthy bout of no-strings-attached sex. She didn't belong to Eddie any more. She belonged to herself. She could give. And she could take without feeling guilty.

"If you've had your say, I suppose now you expect me to leave your house." He played with a lock of her hair. "I admit I'm an ass. I'm not, however, conceited. Just confident."

The bed shook with her laughter. "You're not conceited," she agreed.

He arched an eyebrow. "There's a but in there somewhere." He tipped a finger under her chin. "Or at least a snotty adjective."

She nudged him over on his back and leaned over him. "You, Dan Sullivan, are jealous." She lay back on the bed, hands folded at her waist and sighed, satisfied.

"You're nuts," he blew the two words up into the air.

She leaned over him again. "Am not." She dove in for a hot kiss. When she pulled away, she saw the haze in his eyes and felt sure. "You want me for yourself. Admit it. You don't want me looking at another man."

"You can look all you want." He took her in his arms. "Just save this for me."

Then he demonstrated again, taking all the sweet time he wanted, what he meant for her to save.

They dozed, wrapped together on top of the disheveled bed linens. She had ten years experience sleeping with her ears on high alert for Amy, so the click aroused her—the sound of the mechanism engaging to open the garage door.

She leaped off the bed and put her clothes on in seconds. She scooped up Dan's things and tugged him to his feet. She tossed his clothes into the bathroom that adjoined her bedroom.

"They're home," she declared, panting. "The door to the right opens on the hall. I'll head them off." She nudged him into the bathroom and closed the door behind him.

She raced out of her room and threw the hall closet door open as she heard the back door creak.

"Mom!"

"In the hall, Amy," she called. She pulled out Amy's jacket and held the hanger in her free hand.

"Hi, Mom." Amy ran to her and hugged her waist. Bobbie followed a few steps behind Amy.

"Is that Dan Sullivan's car out front?" Bobbie asked.

"Yes, it is." Molly hoped she didn't sound breathless. "Detective Sullivan brought back your jacket, Amy." She draped the jacket on the hanger and shoved it back in the closet.

"I've been looking everywhere for that. I thought I lost it." Amy smiled. "Where is Uncle Danny?"

The sound of running water came from behind the closed bathroom door. Molly contained the impulse to laugh. "He's using the washroom, sweetie."

Molly took Amy's hand and walked with her toward the kitchen. Bobbie stood in the hall a few minutes before she joined them. Dan wandered into the room a few minutes later.

"Uncle Danny!" Amy ran to him for a hug.

"Hey, squirt. I found your jacket. Must have been riding in the back seat of my car for weeks. Along with some hardened criminals, too. That jacket has been on an adventure."

"Thanks." She giggled.

He squatted down so she could jump on his broad back for a piggyback ride. She clasped her arms around his neck and leaned her head on his shoulder. He stood facing the women with her little legs poking out on either side of him.

"I've got to go. But I was just telling Molly—that's Mom to you, squirt," he said, as he angled his head up to Amy, "that you're all invited to Thanksgiving dinner at Kay's house. Wasn't I, Molly?"

"Um, yes," Molly stammered. "That's so nice of Kay to invite us. We'll have to get back to you."

"She won't take no for an answer." He smiled at her, so full of that conceit he liked to call confidence that Molly wanted to burst out laughing.

"Well, then I guess we accept." She looked to Bobbie and Amy to be sure they were in agreement.

"Great, I'll tell Kay to set the table for three more." He settled Amy back on her feet. "Give me a hug, Missy A, and I'm out of here."

"I'm going to call Kay and see what I can bring." Bobbie walked to the wall phone.

"Give me a few minutes to call and tell her I invited you first." Dan laughed.

"Oh my." Molly touched Dan's sleeve. "Shouldn't you clear this first with her?"

He covered her hand with his. "No need. All are welcome at this feast every year. My whole family will be there. You'll be treated like family, too."

"Well, then, okay," Molly agreed. Bobbie stared at their hands. "We'll see you Thursday."

"And I'll be here at five tomorrow to take you to that wine dinner at *Il Vicinato's* I told you about, Molly." His cocky smile dared her to wiggle out of the invitation. He winked at Bobbie.

Laughter bubbled up in her throat at Bobbie's quizzical expression and Amy's delighted grin, but she squelched it and blurted, "Okay."

She walked out of the kitchen to usher him to the door. He kissed her fast and full force on the lips, making exaggerated the-coast-is-clear motions before and after. He jumped down the three porch steps and swung into his car, his eyes trained on Molly. He drove away with a shave-and-a-haircut riff on his car horn.

She turned back inside and almost knocked Bobbie down, she hovered so close.

"You're going to dinner with Dan?"

"Just a friendly meal." She tugged her spiked hair, then let her telltale hand drop at her side. "It sounds like fun."

"I'll bet it does." Bobbie squinted her eyes and searched Molly's face.

"You look positively glowing today, Molly," Bobbie said. "Have you done something different with your make-up?"

"Really, I do?" She pulled her hair some more. "Must be that new face cream."

She gave Bobbie a hug and spun her in a circle.

****

They squeezed into the barroom of the quaint little restaurant through a haze of cigarette smoke. People passed drinks overhead from the curved wooden bar and talked over each other in a din of voices punctuated with bursts of laughter. Danny clapped a hand on the shoulder of a tall, mustachioed man who wore a starched, white chef's apron tied high over his midriff.

"Eh, Jimmy," Dan belted out with Tony Soprano bravado.

"Danny boy," he belted back. "Who's the pretty lady that you don't deserve?"

Jimmy gave Molly a known-you-for-years hug and kissed each of her cheeks with pontifical flare. "Welcome to *Il Vicinato*."

He circled his arm around her shoulder and led the way up two wooden steps into the main dining room. Artificial Christmas garlands hung from each of the four corners of the rectangular room and met in the center of the ceiling. A huge foil bell dangled in the middle of the garlands. Multi-colored Italian lights blinked along their grassy lengths. Old-fashioned glass-blown ornaments dangled from hooks imbedded in the swags.

The blonde pine floor matched the bottom two thirds of the paneled walls. Above the panels the walls were lined with framed old Chicago black-and-white prints. Buzzer-doorbells screwed into the walls on one side of each table around the room's perimeter made her think of Chicago's gangster history and discreet waiters who would only dare appear when summoned by a bell.

Menu booklets were on the seats of wooden chairs at various sized, white linen, covered tables. Each place setting included six wine glasses from flute to goblet.

"Here's your table, Danny." Jimmy pulled a seat out for Molly. "First course will be served in fifteen minutes. I better get back to the kitchen. Hey, Flo!" He waved a voluptuous forty-something woman over. "Florence will get your drink order."

"I love wine," Molly said as Florence went to get them each a glass of cabernet.

"You're in the right place." Dan picked up the menu. "This is the annual wine tasting dinner. *Il Vicinato* means the neighborhood house in Italian. This area off Western Avenue is the old ethnic Italian neighborhood. There's a real sense of family here and Jimmy never forgets a face. The food is unbelievable and they keep those wine glasses bottomless the whole night."

Molly leaned toward him to read his open menu. Six courses were listed in Italian. She pointed to the first item. "Do you know what that means?"

"Nope, but it doesn't matter. Jimmy, the man I just introduced to you? He's one of the owners. He does all the cooking for this event—likes to surprise everybody with his creations."

An accordion player with weathered olive skin and Bay of Napoli eyes linked his arms into his instrument, and table-hopping, solicited and played requests. A group of eight swayed in their seats at one table and belted out a pitchy version of "That's Amore."

The white-haired musician approached their table and touched the tip of his beret-like cap. "What would Signora like to hear?"

"Al Di La"?" Molly asked shyly. It was a romantic song that she loved. She always dreamed of a honeymoon in Italy, but never got there. She and Eddie were flat broke when they married. They were lucky they could afford a weekend in the Pocono's.

The accordionist performed the song in a respectable baritone. Dan reached both his hands, palms up, towards her and she rested her hands in his. She felt dreamy and elated with the rare night out with an attractive man—a man that for months had figured into her fantasies. And the day before, that fantasy had turned to reality. She sighed with pleasure.

Course followed course paired with glasses of wine ever filled by unobtrusive wine salespeople.

"I'm *loving* this," Molly declared overloud. "Thank you so much for bringing me here." She smacked a kiss on Dan's cheek.

"You're welcome." He laughed and put a hand on his midriff. "There's still the dessert course left and beware. They have a wine that goes with that, too. So pace yourself."

"I'm a little drunk, I think." Molly looked at the glasses in front of her. "How are there five full glasses of wine here? I feel like I've been drinking non-stop for hours."

She reached for a glass of water and took a drink. "So the last time we, uh, talked, you said you've read Nathaniel Hawthorne." She grinned at him. "What else do you like to read?"

"That was some talk we had." He winked. "I read everything. Psychology books, criminal law, crime novels, thrillers, classics, you name it. You?"

"I read aloud a lot of mandatory Harry Potter," she said and smiled at the thought of Amy, "and there's the obligatory medical journals. But what I really love to read are romance novels."

"My wife loves romance novels, too." He lifted her hand to his lips and a warm flutter of his breath warmed her palm. "Any favorite story lines you'd like to reenact with me?"

His casual reference to "his wife" sunk in. She sat back in her chair and pulled her hands out of his with the movement. "Wife." It was a blunt statement that she delivered in a soft voice but it fairly screamed finality.

Unperturbed, he scooped her hands back up and held them both to his lips. "*Ex*-wife. She divorced me ten years ago. You'd think by now I'd remember the 'ex' part."

He bent his head over her hand and lavished it with soft kisses. Rivers of chills ran up her arms and she savored the sensation. He raised his eyes to meet hers. She saw the dark grief simmering beneath the surface of his ocean-green eyes and was troubled. Her instincts told her not to push for personal answers.

"How did you get into police work?"

"I was in the Military Police Airborne. I moved pretty far up the ranks and thought that I would have a military career. But the separations were hard on my marriage and my wife decided she

115

wouldn't stick it out with a soldier. When my tour of duty was over, I didn't re-up. She said she could hack it if I pursued a law enforcement career, especially if I made it to Police Commissioner like my dad. She aspired big. I came home to Chicago and studied at the Police Academy. My major in college was psychology. Turned out I had a knack for criminal profiling, so I gravitated to homicide." His eyes looked weary. "Compared to combat, it's dream work. But not compared to anything else, I suspect."

"You don't enjoy what you do?"

"I've been asking myself that question a lot lately." He paused as their wine glasses were refilled. "I'm probably just frustrated because I can't get a bead on the HH Killer. Here comes dessert. Get ready for ecstasy."

The waiter cleared away the china plates, sprinkled with remnants of pastry crumbs. Although ready to explode, she still found room to sip the candy-sweet dessert wine and mull over Danny's comment, "*She divorced me*".

Maybe it was liquid courage from the diverse wine sampling or maybe it was her recent internal admission that she cared for him that prompted her to learn more. "Danny what happened to end your marriage?"

He put his coffee cup down and she realized for the first time that evening that he hadn't been drinking the wine. Guilty for the misty high she experienced alone, she was grateful for his assuming the designated driver role for her.

"My gosh, I think I'm quite drunk, now." She put her hand to her forehead, rubbed her temples and tried to clear the haze. "I'm sorry to be nosy. You don't have to answer that question about your marriage."

"I don't mind," he said. A wide smile dimpled his cheeks and she caught the wicked gleam in his eyes.

"You're trying to get me drunk so you can take advantage of me."

He laughed. "Hell if I am. I'm just enjoying seeing you…disarmed, instead of having that pole up your ass."

"I…hell, you're right." She smiled, satisfied. She took another sip of her cordial and licked her lips.

He looked amused and then his gaze shifted inward. "My wife served me with divorce papers the day after she cleared out her closet and moved in with her boss. I was on duty so there wasn't any confrontation. She left behind a nice note that spelled things out. No hard feelings and all…"

His words penetrated the wine haze. "Danny, I'm so sorry." She touched his arm.

"It's okay," he replied. "She had a baby seven months later. I was sure he was my boy. She wouldn't agree to a paternity test. Said it was *his*. So I got a lawyer and forced the issue. He wasn't my son. I would have moved heaven and earth to somehow stay together if he were. They moved away a couple of months later."

"My God…" She tried to get her fuzzy head around the magnitude of his loss. She tightened her hand on his arm.

He put his hand over hers. "It was a long time ago. Drink up, lady. Time to get you home."

The chill evening air hit her and made her head spin. She tucked her hand around Dan's bicep, teetered a little on her feet and listed toward him. They made their way to his car, a Herculean Hummer that he described as his pride and joy. She sang along with the James Taylor CD he played on the way home, happy and dizzy with the rush of blurred scenery out the car windows.

"You have a pretty voice, Mol," he said. "I'm too much of a gentleman to point out a few of those words sound slurred, though."

She hiccupped. "Na ah," she protested. "I feel great."

"I'll drop you straight home," he said.

She peered at the digital clock on the dashboard. "It's only 9:30. I told Bobbie I'd be home at 10:30. Maybe we could go to your place?" She slipped her hand into his lap and felt his surge of interest.

"Next time." He cleared his throat. "It would be better if you were fully conscious."

"Aw right," she muttered. Her head drooped and bobbed with the rolling motion of the car.

The rush of cold air woke her from a sound sleep when Dan opened her door.

"Can you walk? Or do you want me to carry you?" He leaned into the car.

"I'm fine." She slid out of the seat and landed in his arms.

"Sure you are." He carried her up the steps leading to her front door and set her on her feet. "Keys?"

She handed him her purse with a loopy swing of her arm.

"Okay for me to look in here?" She didn't protest, so he opened the purse and shoved stuff around until he found keys. He eased her through the door and made sure that she stood solidly in the hall before he grabbed the door handle and stepped back through the threshold.

He leaned inside. "When I close the door, I want you to twist the dead bolt, okay, Molly?"

"'Kay," she said. "Had so much fun tonight."

"Me, too." He brushed a kiss on her lips. "Good thing you're a doctor," he said. "You're going to need one in the morning."

He closed the door and knocked twice when she slid the dead bolt in place.

Chapter 14

On Thanksgiving Day morning Molly snuggled deeper into the velvety flannel sheets on her bed and luxuriated in the softness. Bright rays of sunshine slanted through the white shutter slats on her bedroom windows. She was ready to observe the national day of gratitude with an open heart. She had so much to be thankful for.

Amy thrived in her new surroundings and seemed to have left the morose little girl bereft from her father's death behind in New York. Molly had given herself permission to explore a new beginning with Danny and experiment with love. Her heart would always hold a special, untouchable place for Eddie, but it was time to live again.

Danny had shown her that it was possible. The week before she had taken tentative steps with him. She couldn't believe that she had let loose and drank herself into a first-class hangover on what she now thought of as their first date. She never got drunk. Control was all-important to her. But without any conscious thought she had relinquished control to Danny for just one night. He didn't abuse it, even though his teasing call the next day abused her pounding head. He had called her every day since Sunday and she relished the conversations. Step by step she drew closer to him.

She was about to take another huge step towards a new life. Glad that he had tricked her into accepting his invitation to Kay's for the holiday, she looked forward to a large family dinner and hoped that she would feel accepted in the Sullivan ranks.

She angled an arm over her head and rested it on the pillow. Just a few more minutes in this comfy bed. Her house smelled like chocolate and pumpkin. A shrill whistle blasted and snare drums rolled. She jumped out of bed, shrugged on her terrycloth robe and knotted its belt around her waist when she heard Amy call, "Mom! The parade's starting."

She opened her bedroom door and the enticing fragrance of baking intensified. Bobbie used Kay's recipe for pumpkin bread. She hurried to the back of the house with little-girl anticipation.

A plate piled with slices of warm bread and a tray of mugs filled with hot chocolate were on the coffee table. Amy sat on the floor with her back against the black leather sofa, her legs stretched out beneath the coffee table. She smiled up at Molly with her mouth full and a chocolate mustache painted on her upper lip.

She sat down hip-to-hip with Amy and helped herself to breakfast. They watched the Macy's parade together every year. She didn't have many traditions to treasure from her childhood and she wanted Amy to have very different memories.

Her father, a celebrity plastic surgeon on the West Coast and her mother, a career hostess, didn't celebrate holidays. They entertained them. Molly's remembrances were of the nannies that watched the parade or decorated the tree with her.

She had prayed each year for a brother or sister. Her prayer had been answered when she was ten. It taught her to be careful what you pray for because you just might get it. She wasn't close to her sister. It might have been because of the age difference or because they were leagues apart as people. Her sister was as involved with her New York social life as their parents were in Hollywood circles. Holidays sometimes came and went without any of them acknowledging each other's existence.

She and Eddie had planned to have a large family. Those plans died in an instant. But for the first time in a long time she hoped that her life as a woman didn't end with Eddie's death.

They cocooned in the warmth of their home all morning. After Santa rode into Herald Square, they dressed and piled into the car for the ride to the Lynch house.

Molly's stomach tensed and knotted when they rolled up in front of the stately brick Colonial. Bobbie slammed on the brakes as a football sailed over the roof of the two-story house, thudded on the hood of the jeep, bounced into the street and wobble-rolled to the far curb. The ladies stepped out of the car as a troop of masculinity charged around the side of the house.

Mike Jr. ran behind a buff man with buzz-cut sandy hair in grass-stained sweats. "Nice kick, Uncle Pat. I wish I could kick it over the house like you can," Mikey said, his eyes aglow with hero worship.

"Don't even try it, sport. Your mother will kill me. Hey, finally the pretty ladies are here. They're on my team," he yelled over his shoulder. "Hi, I'm Patrick," he extended a hand to Molly and her family.

Joe jogged around the house in a sweat-soaked, gray sweatshirt, paired with a man who looked like a younger version of him and followed by Danny in identical sweats.

"No way," Joe contended to Patrick. "Bobbie's on

121

my team and I'll flip you for Amy and Doc."

A man with strawberry blonde hair in a *Chicago Bears* sweatshirt ran into the street and scooped up the ball. He trotted back to the front lawn. "I'm Brian and I'll gladly tackle you ladies anytime."

"Me, too," the Joe look-alike said. "I'm Jimmy." He shook hands, grinning.

****

Dan strode up in time to rescue the women, although from the admiring looks on their faces, he wasn't too sure that they wanted to be rescued.

He draped his arm possessively around Molly's shoulder. "The only one tackling Molly will be me." He lowered his head and gave her a slow, gentle kiss. He smiled at the crimson blush that crept from her neck to her face at Amy's and his brothers' catcalls.

"Hi. I'm glad you came," Danny said. He tugged her closer to his chest when he felt her slight pull back. *We're a demonstrative bunch and the prissy little doctor needs to get used to it.*

Molly glanced at Amy and Bobbie's elated faces and Dan felt her muscles relax beneath his hand. She smiled at them, then up at him. "I'm glad we came, too."

Her smile sparked a soft, sapphire glow in her round eyes that shot an arrow straight to his heart. What was it about her that pulled him closer each time he saw her and made him miss her during the daily routines that once satisfied him?

****

The front door opened and Molly pulled quickly away from him at the sight of the regal, older woman. She wore lavender, an Eileen Fisher pantsuit that looked stunning on her diminutive figure. The color complimented her shiny, white hair and fair complexion. Her makeup was subtle and impeccable. Just a touch of gray shadow highlighted her blazing blue eyes and a splash of pink blush emphasized high cheekbones.

"Boys, that's enough," she said in a muted voice. "I want you in this house, changed and presentable in ten minutes. Your sister could use your help."

She walked down the steps toward them. Five grown men and one little boy jumped to attention.

Dan tossed Molly a muffled aside. "Here comes Mrs. Sullivan — that blue-eyed blonde I told you about."

She stretched out her hand. "Hello. I'm Jean Sullivan. You must be Molly. And Bobbie. Welcome. Kay's in the kitchen getting an unwanted lesson in how to properly baste a turkey from her father. Please come in."

She turned to Amy. "Amy love, how are you? My goodness, you've grown a foot since the last time I saw you. I've missed you."

Amy flew into Jean's outstretched arms and put her entire little body into the hug. "I missed you too, Grandma. Is Mary in the kitchen?"

"Of course she is. I think she's waiting for you to help her set the table."

Astonished as Amy and Mrs. Sullivan walked arm and arm into the house, Molly looked at Dan.

Amusement twinkled in his eyes. "She may be little but that woman packs quite a wallop."

"I like the way she makes all you big rugged men turn into boys again," Bobbie remarked. She smiled up at Joe as he put his arm around her shoulder.

Dan took Molly's hand. "Come on, let's go. I'm starving and the game should be starting soon."

He guided her into the front hall past the spacious living room. Butter cream colored walls were stenciled with mauve filigree swirls and pineapples below cherry crown moldings. A mahogany, Steinway grand piano hulked near the bay window. Eclectic groupings of antique Victorian furniture atop bold-colored Persian area rugs were juxtaposed with brass floor lamps and large floral accent pieces. There was a pile of blocks on one carpet and a battered plastic tricycle in one corner.

The cornucopia Kay made with Mary graced a large glass coffee table with brass legs. "Looks nothing like mine," Molly observed with a rueful smile.

Her cell phone trilled and she reached into her purse. She glanced at Dan. "Sorry. I have to take this. I'm on call." She listened, nodded and gazed ahead, focusing on the dispatcher's rapid-fire information.

"I have to go to the hospital. There are multiple injuries coming in. I'm sorry, Danny. Let me find Amy and Bobbie and make my apologies to Kay."

She followed him to the kitchen.

Kay bent over the open oven door and almost touched foreheads with a white-haired man in precisely creased khaki trousers and a navy blue sweater. "Daddy if you don't put that spoon down and get out of my kitchen in one minute you'll be sorry."

"Darlin', I'm just trying to show you the right way to baste a turkey."

They stood up together and almost conked heads. "You touch that oven door one more time, Daddy, and you're going to need a doctor. Hi Molly. I think my dad will need you in a few minutes."

Mr. Sullivan looked at Danny, lime eyes twinkling, before he offered his hand to Molly. "Pleasure to meet you, Molly."

"Glad to meet you, too, Mr. Sullivan," she said.

"Please call me John."

"Of course. I'm afraid that Mike will have to doctor you, John, after Kay beats you with the turkey baster. I just got paged to the ER. I have to go. I'm so sorry to miss dinner, Kay."

"Nothing to be sorry about. We're all used to emergencies here. Come back when you can. I'll keep a plate warm for you."

Kay nudged the oven door closed with her foot and the homey smell of roasted turkey abated. "Go ahead, Molly. I'll let Amy know where you are and that you'll be back as soon as you can."

Danny encircled her shoulders with his arm. "Let me walk you to your car."

The air outside smelled peppery from burnt wood and the wind dragged sooty plumes of smoke away from the house's brick chimney in a trail of ragged clouds.

Dan opened Molly's car door for her. "Want me to drive you? I can put on my siren and get you there really fast."

"Thanks, but I've got time. Some high school football players decided to celebrate their victory today with a drag race on Mack Road."

"Dead Man's Curve. I know it well."

"They're pulling one car out of the pond and pulling kids out of another car wrapped around a tree. I'm not sure how many casualties there are or the extent of injuries, but I should beat the ambulances."

"Come back no matter how late." He leaned toward her and gave her a sweet, warm kiss that made her hungry to stay. He closed the door and tapped the roof of her car.

He watched her progress down the quiet street lined on both sides with leafless trees until he could no longer see the taillights of her car. He stood a few minutes in the early dusk and felt alone even with a house full of family behind him. He missed her. And looked forward to seeing her again when her job was done. He recognized the long suppressed feelings of expectance, desire and hopefulness she evoked. *I'm in trouble. I've got it bad.*

He didn't hear his mother come up behind him until she spoke, "She's the one, Danny?"

He thought about his wedding day and felt a tug of sadness. "I thought Carly was the one, Ma." He turned and offered his mother his arm to hold.

She slipped her hand into the crook of his elbow and they walked back toward the house.

****

Molly tried to erase the past few hours from her mind during the trip back to the Lynch home. Healthy teenagers, careless in their abuse of alcohol and delusions of immortality created a nightmare reality in the ER. Two young men died, two clung to life and one faced a life confined in a wheelchair. Tears of frustration and sympathy for the parents welled in her eyes. She blinked them back and focused on her driving and the thought of the welcoming family who awaited her return.

Danny greeted her at the door before she got her hand up to ring the bell. His brow furrowed and she suspected she looked as pathetic as she felt. He enfolded her in his arms and she wanted to stay there, half in Kay's door and let the waves of pleasure drown everything else inside her.

"I'm sorry I'm so late."

"It's okay. I'm glad you made it back." He clasped her hand and led her toward the dining room that blazed with light and buzzed with banter.

Half the clan sat around the table. Mike Lynch and John Sullivan officiated at each head. Ravished platters and food-smeared dishes made Kay's elegant dining room look like a horde of barbarians had fought and conquered.

"We kept a plate warm for you." Kay's bright eyes turned pensive as she looked at Molly. "How about a cup of tea and a piece of pumpkin pie instead?"

"That would be great. Thanks, Kay." Molly sat on the chair that Danny pulled out for her and he sat next to her. A low-grade headache and the glare of light from the crystal chandelier over the table made her squint her eyes. She felt unraveled and unsociable.

Before Kay could get up from the table, Mrs. Sullivan bustled out of the kitchen carrying a plate of pie and a cup with a dangling tea bag string. She handed the food across the table to Molly and took a seat.

"Thank you so much, Mrs. Sullivan. I'm sorry to be a bother."

"No bother at all dear. I'm glad you were able to come back tonight. I was looking forward to meeting you. I want to thank you for taking such good care of Danny. I'm sure he wasn't an easy patient."

Molly half snorted a laugh. "So true. He fought me every chance he got."

"Yes, that sounds like my Danny. But he's a good boy."

"Ma…," Danny groaned.

"All you men go in the den and yell at umpires. I would like to talk to the lady who seems to have taken a bit of Danny's heart."

All eyes turned towards Molly. She snapped her head in Danny's direction. She couldn't read his expression. Did he agree with his mother? *Good God was she going to talk with Jean Sullivan about her son's heart?*

"Daniel, scram."

"Yes ma'am. But be kind, Ma. No little boy or toilet training stories, okay? Don't scare her off."

His mother shot him a move-it look and he abandoned Molly to the unnerving interview. Mr. Sullivan, apparently as obedient to his wife as their children, followed his sons and son-in-law out of the room.

"Now, Molly." Mrs. Sullivan stared at her evenly. "I understand that you don't like police officers. Why not?"

Uncomfortable with the abrupt question, Molly collected her thoughts before she answered. "It's not that I don't like what Danny does—what you're whole family does. On the contrary, I respect and admire the profession. I was married to a police officer, too, Mrs. Sullivan. It wasn't just a job to Eddie. It was what defined him. He was utterly fearless. And I wasn't. I'm not. I'm very reluctant to face the daily fear again. I felt like I gave my husband over to the force. How have you done that with your husband and all your children?"

"I never gave them to the force. It's more like I lend them." She chuckled. "Don't think I don't worry about my family. I pray every day for their safety and happiness. But much as I want to hold and protect them, they're in God's hands, not mine. I have to believe that they'll lead the life that He plans for them. Believe me. My heart stops when the phone rings late at night, but my faith keeps me going. How do you think those young football players' parents felt when the phone rang today?"

"It was a parent's nightmare." Molly scooped the tea bag up with a spoon, twisted the string to drain it and set it on her pie plate.

Jean nodded. "I'm sure they worried needlessly all through the game that their sons might be injured on the field. Look what happened anyway. They were blind-sided with tragedy. You can't worry about things you can't control. I'm sure you didn't worry about your husband when he went out to the store. No. You worried he would be hurt at work and that never happened."

"Danny told you about Eddie's death?"

"Yes he did, dear." She reached across the table and touched Molly's hand. "I'm not trying to push my son on you. But I think he has strong feelings for you. You're the only woman he's introduced to our family since his divorce. Since I'm quite sure he hasn't lived like a monk, much as I'd like to pretend he has, this tells me a lot about the extent of his feelings for you. If you should have similar feelings... Well. Don't let what Dan does for a living cloud what you feel for him as a man."

"Thank you. I appreciate your advice. I'm starting to see what a caring, thoughtful man you raised."

"He's a thoughtful, generous man who has been badly hurt. I don't want to see him hurt again."

Molly noted the tacit warning behind her gentle voice.

She winked at Molly. "Now, Molly, did you know that Danny was so nervous the first day of school he wet his pants not once but twice?"

Dan appeared in the dining room archway. "Mother?"

Jean stood and touched his cheek. "Why don't you see Molly home? We've had such a nice talk." She gave Molly a warm, maternal hug.

"I don't think Bobbie and Amy are ready to leave," Danny said. "Bobbie and Joe are in the middle of a chess game and Mary wants Amy to sleep over."

"I'll go check on them," Molly offered.

"Why don't you two just head out? I'll let everyone know you've left."

"Thanks, Mom."

"Yes, thanks. It's been a pleasure meeting you."

"I've enjoyed it, too. Now scoot."

****

There she is. Isn't she beautiful? I want to touch her silky, golden hair.

"Can I help you?"

Is she talking to me? I look around and no one

129

else is at the counter. She is. She is talking to me. I can't believe it.

"Are you interested in the colognes?"

I force myself to answer. "Yes. Yes I am. I like the smell of flowers."

"Who doesn't? I love these fragrances. They last a long time, too. I wear them all the time."

She likes me. She wants to be my girlfriend. "Which one is your favorite?"

"My favorite is the Lily of the Valley. I have it on today. Here, smell. Isn't it pretty?"

I lean down and sniff her wrist. I have never been close enough to smell anyone's wrist before. I like it. I like being close to my girlfriend. She smells just like a garden.

"Is this for your girlfriend?"

"No. I don't have a girlfriend."

"A Christmas present for your mom?"

"Yes. It is a gift for my mother."

"What a great son your are. Your mother will love the Lily of the Valley."

"Yes. I am a good son."

"You can take this to the front register and pay with the rest of your groceries."

"Thank you. Thank you very much."

She likes me. She treats me special. I don't want to leave. I want to stay with her. I have her perfume now. I can smell her anytime I want.

I push my cart past her counter one more time to look at her.

Who's that with her now? What are you doing, Ma? Don't talk to my girlfriend. Don't ruin this for me. What are you saying to my girlfriend? You are telling her lies, aren't you? I saw you buy her perfume, too. You can't have it. I am going to kill you for this, Ma. I am going to kill you again and again.

I follow behind your car and you pretend you don't see me. But you know I am here.

You ruined everything. You will never talk to my girlfriend again. She's mine. As soon as you get out of your car, I will make you sorry.

I hate you. I hate you. I leave my car and I'm behind you before you know what is happening. You will pay. I grab your hair and my knife slices across your neck. Your flaming hair feels coarse against my fingers. Not soft. Different.

I pull but it comes off in my hand in a lump. I don't understand. There is brown hair under the red. You are not my mother. What have I done? I am sorry.

I am sorry, pretty lady. You will be all right. Here. Smell this. I will spray your wrist just like my girlfriend.

Look what you made me do, Ma. I know you are watching me. You made me do this. I see you watching me through that camera. I am coming for you. I am coming. You will pay for this.

Chapter 15

Molly's eyebrow arched as Danny steered her to the shiny black Lexus sedan. "Wow. What a gorgeous car."

"Like it?"

"Where's the Hummer?"

"In my garage. My one addiction. Love this car. She drives like a dream."

She sank into the butter-soft, black leather and sighed. "This is decadent. I don't think you should seek help for your addiction."

The car purred and glided out of the driveway. She leaned her head back on the headrest and sighed again.

She looked so deflated and tiny in the roomy seat. "Tough one?"

"Lately, they've all been tough ones."

"I know just the place to make you feel better."

He turned the radio on to a light music station and Elton John's *Candle In the Wind* filled the car's cabin from twelve different speaker positions. She sang along in a pretty soprano and he smiled remembering her slurry sing-along after the wine dinner.

Fifteen minutes later she hiked up in her seat and looked out the window as the car lurched over bumps on a tree-lined path. "Where are we?"

"You'll see."

He stopped on the crown of a low hill. The Chicago skyline spread before them in the far distance like sparkling steps and stairs. The stars glittered in a dome over flat terrain. The Sears Tower, alight in autumn orange, dominated the horizon and speared the clear, blue-black sky.

"Where are we? This is amazing. How did you ever find this?" She looked at him, her eyes round and shining.

"I grew up near here. All the teenagers know about this make-out place. We're a little early. We have it to ourselves."

He undid his seatbelt, then hers. He fiddled with his seat lever and rode his seat back as far as it went. "Sit on my lap?"

"You're kidding?" She stared at him and he didn't respond. "You're not kidding?" She grinned at him and her eyes danced with mischief. "It's been forever since I did anything like this. My luck we'll get caught."

She slipped over the console and her petite body straddled him with ease. His stomach clenched and he hardened beneath her soft haunches.

"Are you sure you haven't done this lately?" He shifted beneath her and hardened even more.

"It's like riding a bike." She laughed and used her teeth to nip at his bottom lip.

"Lady, you have no idea what you're doing to me."

"Oh, I have a clue. Got an A in anatomy."

She ground her body slow and seductive on his lap. Their eyes locked in the shadows as he unbuttoned her coat. She unbuttoned his shirt. He undid the buttons of her blouse and pressed his mouth to the vee of her cleavage. He lingered there and slid her bra straps over each shoulder. Slowly he drew the delicate material down to expose each breast.

She ran her hands over his chest and arched her neck back as he applied gentle suction to each nipple. He feasted on her sweetness and was unbearably aroused by her reaction. He pitched his hips up so he could dig under her bottom and unzip his pants. They wiggled out of any clothes that barred intimate access.

He needed to be inside her. He clasped her waist and lifted her astride him. She gasped as he entered her. The sound of her passion touched his soul and set every nerve ending on fire.

She rode him slow, up and down, her head thrown back. Her soft hands foraged under his shirt, over his chest and arms like molten silk pouring over him. They moved together in perfect unison, holding and prolonging the powerful sensations that swelled between them, through them, until they lost control. They pumped in a frenzy gasping for air. Their lips met and their tongues collided muffling their ecstatic cries. Her body went lax still astride him and she uttered a satisfied groan.

He saw pinpoints of light on his closed lids. "Wow," the word gushed from his lips. He held her as she snuggled against his chest, both trembling in the aftermath.

"I hear bells," she said.

"Honey, I hear bells, too. I think it's your phone."

His cell phone rang and they pulled back to look at each other.

"This can't be good news." He kissed her before he helped her slide off his lap, mostly naked and tantalizing, into her seat. She dove for her purse.

They both dealt with the calls while they

grabbed their clothes and wiggled into them.

He fished an emergency beacon out of his glove compartment and set it on the top of his car. The rotating light washed the grass and tree limbs with red swirls.

"He's hit again," he said as he started the car. "We've got a live victim on the Eisenhower Expressway five minutes away from Chicago Regional."

"I know," she said. "They're trying to patch me in to the paramedics now."

He thrust the gearshift into reverse, tossed his arm over his seat and floored the accelerator. "Seat belt on?"

She nodded.

He backed the car down the path full tilt. Seatbelts strained as the impacts from the bumpy road jolted them in their seats. The tires hit asphalt and he slammed on the brakes. All the anti-skid devices in the car engaged with a mechanical moan and they fishtailed onto the road. He floored the car again and they took off.

He wanted to tell her what their trip to lovers lane meant to him. But there'd be time for that later. *Not now.* He could only think one thing. *A break. This could be the break I need to stop the bastard.*

Her calm voice on the phone played over the background sounds of the radio as he wove among the sparse cars on the expressway, and thanked God for the V-8 engine that blasted them down the road over a hundred miles per hour.

"They're there," she said as she snapped her phone shut. "My team's ready for her."

"I need you to keep her alive."

"I'll do my best."

****

Dan gunned the sleek car down the exit ramp and left Molly's stomach somewhere on the highway behind them. At one point all four tires spun on air at the same time. Like a car chase scene in an action adventure, they blew through every red light and ignored any speed limitations. They had to get to the hospital before it was too late.

The ambulance bay was an impenetrable wall of emergency vehicles that threw off spinning light like crazy, mirrored balls. Danny drove the car as close to the door as he could on pavement, then swerved and drove on the lawn almost up to the building foundation.

They both swung their doors wide and left them gaping open the instant he slammed on the brakes. Speed was everything. They sprinted into the ER, through the waiting room and into the trauma treatment area.

They didn't slow down as the desk clerk anticipated the question and yelled out, "Trauma one, Dr. Jordan."

They charged through the doors of trauma one together. Trudy held out a paper, surgical coat. Molly walked into it and let the tie strings hang down her back. She grabbed gloves from the wall dispenser, stretched them on and stepped into the bloody scene, Danny at her elbow.

"We're losing her," were the first words from a trauma team member.

She positioned herself across from her colleague who attempted to stem the blood flow from a shoulder-to-shoulder transverse wound. The long slash was shallow enough to have missed arteries. But Molly knew it didn't matter. They wouldn't be able to compensate for the rapid blood loss. Still, they'd try.

"Airway's clear. Can we get a clamp on this?" Her fingers pinched bloody flesh.

Danny hung over her. "Molly, let me in there. She may be able to tell me something."

"No."

"What's her name?" he demanded to the room.

"Liza. Liza Dean."

"Liza," he called out. He was so close to Molly that his breath tickled the back of her neck. "I'm Detective Sullivan. Who did this to you? Talk to me, Liza. I want to catch him. Who did this?"

"Detective Sullivan, I can't have you in here. She can't talk," Molly snapped at him.

He persisted. "Liza!"

Liza's eyelids flittered and her lips pursed. She blew the tiniest expiration.

"What? Liza what?" Danny leaned over the woman's head, urgent, tensed.

Molly tried to nudge him away. "Sullivan, for God's sake!"

"Fflrrr...." Liza's face went slack.

"She's diving," Trudy said, her eyes fixed on machine gauges.

Molly shouted over the clamor of the monitors' warning alarms. "*Move*, Detective. Start compressions."

He stepped back and Molly worked. An iridescent green flat-line on the heart monitor persisted.

"Paddles," Molly called.

They tried to bring Liza back three times before Molly ordered compressions to stop and pronounced the time of her death. Trudy turned off the machines and the deflated, blood-splattered group stood in eerie silence around Liza's ravaged corpse.

Molly swiveled her head and looked into Danny's stricken eyes. "I'm sorry, Danny."

He nodded.

She turned back to her team. "Family outside?"

"Not that we've been told."

"Okay."

"Molly I've got to get to the scene," Danny

137

informed her. "Can you get a ride?"

She ripped off her paper gown and pulled off her surgical gloves. "I'll go with you."

"No—"

"I'll sit in the car." She walked to his side. "I won't get in the way."

He nodded and they left trauma one. They walked outside into a beehive of law enforcement personnel who paced, leaned against trucks and cars or guarded the ER entrance to prevent camera crew access. Danny spotted Joe and Barnes and strode over to them.

He shook his head in answer to the question in their eyes. "Where'd they find her?"

"West Loop off of Monroe. Condo garage," Joe said.

"No use waiting around here now," Barnes said. "I guess we'll go over to the scene."

"No. I'll go. You guys can go home."

They climbed into his car. Danny backed the Lexus off the lawn and left deep ruts in the car's wake. The crime scene was less than ten minutes away from the hospital.

Dan stopped at a red light, no need to rush.

"It feels like him, but it can't be," he said. "Why would he break pattern?"

"Did you see her hair?" Molly asked. "She was brunette."

"Yeah, I saw. And why the city? Why at night? Doesn't add up."

They pulled off Monroe and rolled up to a cordoned-off area. Danny hung his arm out the window, his police identification in his hand. He parked in an alley behind the building in front of two open garage doors and got out of the car. Lights blazed within and outside, just beyond his car.

The glare ahead of Molly made the darkness seem deeper where she sat. She gestured for Danny to go ahead when he turned back toward her. He crouched under the yellow tape stretched between the doors and disappeared inside.

She cuddled inside her coat against the luxurious leather seat. Danny had left the keys in the ignition and she could always turn on the heater if she got cold or switch on the radio if she got bored. She didn't care how long she'd have to sit there alone. She didn't feel alone tonight.

Mrs. Sullivan had said she had taken a bit of Danny's heart. She didn't tell his mother that Danny had stolen her heart. It was true. And for the first time since Eddie started his job on the police force, she felt fearless.

Chapter 16

Danny found the murder scene on the second level of the garage. The forensic team was going over every inch of a battered, dull-gold Toyota Corolla with its trunk open. An irregular trail of smeared blood stained the concrete floor beneath the rear bumper of the car. One of his counterparts appeared to be in charge.

Danny walked over to him. "Detective Dan Sullivan, Windsor precinct."

"Greg Morris," he said, extending a beefy hand. "What brings you downtown?"

"Thought this was the serial killer case I've been working on, but it's not his MO," Danny said. "Might be a copy cat."

"You working the HH Killer case?"

Danny nodded.

"Then this is your perp all right. Hey, Billy. Show Detective Sullivan what we pulled out of the dumpster."

Billy backed out of the car holding a plastic bag. He handed it to Danny. It contained a tangled, auburn red wig.

"Okay, red hair," Danny said soberly. "Liza

Dean—the vic—a housewife?"

"Nope, single. But she was out grocery shopping. Check out the trunk," Greg said.

Only a handful of homicide officers knew the details of the previous murders. The victims were found locked in the trunks of their cars. Their throats were cut so deep they were near decapitated. Deep crisscrossed X's were slashed across both eye sockets, then the bodies were shoved in among grocery bags. None of that had ever been released to the press to prevent copycat killings.

Nobody had seen or heard anything during murders that up until then had taken place during workdays in suburban neighborhoods. More than half the population in those areas was made up of nine-to-fivers who were at work when prior murders had occurred. No murder weapon had been recovered. The killer left behind no prints, skin or hair. Footprint analyses hadn't told them anything. None of the supermarket personnel they had interviewed tied the victims with anyone else they'd seen at the stores. Neighborhood canvasses had been fruitless. No apparent connection had figured in to the almost ritualistic slashings. They had nothing.

But if this was his guy, he had deviated. That might be something.

Danny crouched down near the bloodstains and examined the cement floor. *Was that what Liza was trying to say? Floor?* He looked up around the garage structure.

"Can I get the security tape from that camera?" He asked Greg, pointing at one of the overhead steel beams where a camera perched.

"Sure, but probably won't do you any good. The camera was blown."

"How?"

"Shot out. We have the bullet from a thirty-eight."

141

"Anybody question the security guard?"

"Yeah. He's downstairs at the lobby desk. Told him to stick around."

"Thanks." Dan stood up and watched the forensics guys work. "Liza Dean died at Chicago Regional about a half hour ago. I'll make sure you get the Medical Examiner's report."

"Yeah, good. I have a team canvassing the area starting with residents here. Maybe we'll pick up something."

"Thanks, Greg." Danny exchanged business cards with the Chicago detective. "I'll go check with that guard for the tape."

Maybe the killer lives here. Something must have happened to make him leave her. Maybe someone walked or drove in. We may have a witness.

****

Molly snapped awake from a light doze when she heard the car door open. "Hi." She straightened in her seat. "Did that go well?"

He slouched in the seat next to her, his arms straight ahead of him on the wheel. "It's him. And so far, I'm nowhere with this."

He turned his face to her and she tried to make out his features in the dim light. She felt tremendous empathy for him after all that they had shared that evening. How had they gone from a radiant teenage romp in a parked car to a dark alley a short distance away from a murder scene? She had failed tonight. And she knew Danny felt the same way.

"You'll get him. He'll make a mistake," she reassured him.

"He will." He started the car and drove into the street. "Maybe he already has. What do you think Liza was trying to tell us? Sounded like floor."

"I know. Does it make sense to you?"

"None at all. Except that's where they found her.

On the garage floor."

They sped along the highway both lost in thought.

"Could have been 'Florida' or 'Florsheim'. Maybe he wore a sweatshirt or something. Or even his shoes?" She itched to get her hands on a dictionary and just go down the list of possibilities.

He shook his head. "I just don't know."

"She was so young," she lamented. "So sweet to be brutalized that way. I can still smell her perfume. Lily of the Valley. I love that flower. I have scads of them in my garden."

He was silent. She didn't blame him. But she wanted to connect with him and help him somehow. "Danny, when we get to my house, do you want to come in and have a cup of coffee or a drink or something?"

"I can't. I have to get down to the station and look at a security tape."

"I understand." She sat quietly and tried to think of something she could say to demonstrate that she cared about his work. She did care. It occurred to her that it was because she cared for him.

"Thank you for Thanksgiving, Danny. And for…later. This, now, only makes the first part of today seem that much more special to me. I'm very thankful I met you."

He reached across the console for her hand and pressed it to his lips. The intimate gesture moved her and made her want her arms around him, to console, to caress, to make up for the memory of lives cut short that night.

"Come back to me tonight whenever you're done. Stay with me," she said.

"I don't know how long I'll be." He rested her hand on his thigh and covered it with his. "I'll probably be lousy company anyway."

"It doesn't matter." She pulled her hand out from under his and brushed it down the side of his face. His eyes closed for a moment at her touch. "I want to be with you."

He stopped the car in her driveway. "I'll come back later," he promised.

She slipped her house key into his hand. "The security code is 1010973. Want me to write it down for you?"

He shook his head and smiled.

"Okay. See you later."

****

Several weary homicide cops clustered around the monitor in the station house's meeting room. Danny rewound and played the tape again. He saw the upturned head covered by the dark ski mask. The man's mouth formed several words. Then a pistol loomed in front of the lens and the picture blanked.

He rewound again and paused the tape for several frames where the view of the killer's eyes and mouth were best. The angle of the camera distorted his image so that it was impossible to determine much about the man's body. His eyes appeared light gray in the black and white image and what skin was exposed in the mask looked light enough for him to be Caucasian. He hoped the computer guys could come up with something useful.

He looked at the killer's teeth bared while he spoke. The ugly grimace showed grayish rot in the mouth. Maybe that would help identify him.

Danny stared at the grotesque visage frozen on the screen. "Did the lip reader make any progress yet?"

"Should have. I'll go see," one of the men offered.

Danny turned off the power on the VCR and rubbed his eyes. He took a seat at the conference room table and jotted down some notes on a yellow-lined pad. His stomach felt hollow, his Thanksgiving pig-out long since burned off by hours of adrenaline-filled action. And there was the acrobatic lovemaking with Molly.

He smiled despite the gnawing professional frustration he felt. She waited for him. The accomplished, complicated, lovely woman waited for him. For all the failure he felt with the events of that night, he thought he was lucky.

The lip reading expert entered the room. Married to one of his junior officers, the young woman volunteered her time whenever they needed her. She was hearing impaired and Danny signed, "Hello. Have you got something for me?"

"Yes," she said in a slow cadence. She blushed deep red. "I'm embarrassed to say it."

"All right…" Sensitive to her distress, he tore a sheet of paper off his pad. He handed her the paper and a pen. "Can you write it down for me instead?"

She scribbled a few words on the paper and folded it in half. She handed it to Danny and said, "Good night, Lieutenant Sullivan." She rushed out of the room.

Danny unfolded the paper and spread it out on the table. His men leaned in around him to read the neatly written phrase in feminine cursive. "Die You Carrot Topped Cunt".

"Nice. The bastard." Guilty that he had asked a sweet lady to communicate such filth, Danny looked at his men.

"Leak that one to the press," spit out one of them. "Fucking HH Killer. Now they can have their CC Killer and the censors will bleep them out every time they say it."

They laughed bawdily and released some abashed tension.

"We've got to get a handle on the way this went down," Danny said, the ring of authority in every word. He picked up the remote control, switched on the TV and played the tape again.

"He blew the camera after he slashed her." Danny paused the tape and walked to the screen. He pointed to the open trunk of the car. He rewound and re-played the tape. "She parks and pops her trunk. You can see shadows move behind there, but the trunk screened the whole thing.

"Was he waiting for her to drive in? How did he know she would? Was he tailing her? Check out the store where she went grocery shopping tonight. We'll want their security tapes. Interview personnel. The neighborhood canvas turned up nothing so far. Let's get Liza Dean's background. Why was she wearing a wig? See if the Medical Examiner got any evidence from Liza's body. I'm going to check a few things here first, then I'll go back out to the scene myself."

Danny walked over to his desk and pulled his bottom drawer open. He shuffled the contents around until he found a dog-eared Webster's dictionary. He flipped to the "fl's".

****

Danny drove into Molly's hushed neighborhood at three in the morning. He cut the engine at the curb and coasted the rest of the way into her driveway. He parked the car and hurried into her house, since he felt vaguely sneaky to enter a woman's home at this hour.

When he opened the front door, he heard a rhythmic beeping sound that emanated from the security keypad on the wall at the left side of the foyer near her bedroom. He tapped in the code and the house was silent. He pulled off his shoes, left them on the area rug in front of her door and walked on the balls of his feet into her room.

Two windows faced west and a sickle moon hung low in the sky, framed perfectly in the clear eyebrow window next to her bed. A swatch of pale lemon light shimmered on her covers and caught the ends of her hair, making them glow on the pillow. She lay on her side, faced away from him, a tiny curvy bundle beneath the billowy, down comforter.

His chest ached with tenderness as he stood at the foot of her bed and watched her sleep. Desire flooded him and he shuddered in its grip. He stripped off his clothes and eased into bed. She stirred and rolled onto her back. He hung over her captivated by the moon-glow on her face.

Her lips parted and he covered them with his. "Molly darling. I'm here," he whispered.

****

Her hands caressed the rippled, muscular chest, brushing over silky hair. She thrilled at the contrast of her soft skin against taut, male flesh. His rough hands pulled the front of her pajamas open and sent a spray of buttons clacking on the floor on either side of the bed. He pushed the cloth off her shoulders. Her nipples swelled and hardened as the cool air brushed against her naked skin. Fire charged through her awakening body as he closed his moist mouth over one breast. He clasped her body closer as he feasted on that breast, then the other. Her stomach clenched as his head moved unhurried, lower, covering every inch of her torso. She moved beneath his lips in involuntary waves. The stubble of his beard scraped against her ribs. His teeth clasped the waistband of her pajama pants and inched them down. Her legs parted as if she had no choice. Her mind was capable of only one thought. "More. Dan, give me more," she moaned.

"I will, darling," he answered.

As he filled her, her waking mind understood that she wasn't dreaming. He rocked her beneath him and pressed her so close that she became a part of his body. He wasn't a fantasy. He was here. He was hers. She was his.

Her body answered the movement of his, building faster, driving, writhing to an orgasm so shattering, it swelled from her fingertips and toes. Drained, he lay with his head between her breasts. She stroked his hair, her mind a perfect blank of contentment.

"I tried to wait up for you," she said. "But I must have fallen asleep. I'm sorry."

"That's okay. It's late, almost morning."

He rolled off of her and cradled her with one arm. She rested her head on his shoulder and straddled one of his legs with hers. Her body molded against his side.

His hand ran up and down her upper arm. She felt cherished and safe. "Did you make any progress with the case?"

"Some. I'm beat."

She looked up into his face. His eyes were closed and she thought of the first time she saw him in the recovery room months ago. He still looked vulnerable. "Sleep," she whispered.

"Mmmm…"

"Good night, Danny." She propped on her elbow and kissed his lips.

"Good night, darling."

She shivered with pleasure at the endearment. She slipped away from the circle of his arm and lay on her pillow. His breathing deepened and she thought he slept.

She closed her eyes. "I love you, Danny," she whispered.

The bed jolted and he was on top of her. His body pressed hers down into the mattress.

"Say it again, Molly. Look at me and say it again."

She met his eyes and searched them. They gleamed with intensity, a stormy, green sea that challenged her. She didn't waver. "I love you."

The storm in his eyes calmed and a smile stretched on his lips. "I love you, too."

He dove in for a kiss and set her aflame again. When they finally slept, they tangled together in a satisfied coma.

Two hours later, Molly disentangled from the cocoon of his arms. She whispered in his ear, "Danny, I have to leave for work. Sleep as long as you want."

He grunted and rolled over.

While she showered and dressed she felt like she floated above the floor. She climbed the stairs and stopped outside Bobbie's bedroom door. She rapped on it and cracked it open. "Bobbie? It's Molly. Can I come in?"

"Um. Sure."

She sat on the edge of Bobbie's bed. "What time are you supposed to pick up Amy, sweetie?"

Bobbie brushed a long tendril of hair away from her mouth. "About ten."

"Okay. But can you make sure Danny's gone by then? I have to go to work and he's still sleeping."

"What? Sleeping where?" Bobbie turned onto an elbow and stared at her.

"Downstairs in my room."

Molly giggled at her stunned expression.

"Holy shit." Bobbie sat up in bed. "Details, boss. I want details."

"No time." Molly patted Bobbie's shoulder and got up to leave.

"Well, it's about time," Bobbie said.

"Yes," Molly beamed at her. "Yes, it is."

Chapter 17

Molly loved him. It was a fact. She had told him so twice, first in a whisper and again, as she looked him straight in the eyes. He believed her the first time she had said it. But when her eyes met his and she professed it once more, he couldn't believe the thrill he felt deep in his soul.

Dan lay in her soft bed and smiled. He had admitted that he loved her, too. And gave her the words along with his heart. There was no turning back.

"I love Molly Jordan." He said it aloud, amazed.

Even with the lack of sleep, he felt alive and refreshed as he let the hot water pound on his back in her shower. Her scent rose along with the steam and made his body throb with need.

There was no end to wanting her. Never enough. He missed her already. He had to find a way for them to be together again that night.

He hummed tunelessly and lingered in the shower while he thought about a future that included her. He wanted and needed Molly in his life. Days that would begin and end with her could make him happy no matter what filled them in

150

between.

But first things first. He had a killer to stop. He needed to get back to work.

Past one o'clock, he plopped a box of doughnuts next to the coffee pot in the squad room. It would be another long day and night before he could steep himself in lilacs and lovemaking.

"Morning, Lieutenant." Nick greeted him and nabbed a jelly doughnut. "Thanks for the breakfast. Or is this lunch? What time is it anyway?"

"Officially, afternoon."

"I thought you were off today." Nick polished off the doughnut and reached for another.

"No days off for anyone until the HH son of a bitch is caught. Where is everybody?"

Danny poured himself a mug of murky coffee and sampled it despite its acrid, faintly burnt smell. "This stuff is poison. Anything new? Any leads?"

"Johnston and Parker are at the parking lot checking through the old tapes and receipts. Residents use a transponder and the public has to take tickets from a dispenser. McKenzie and O'Toole are checking license plates and tracking down the owners. Barnes is here helping me look at cell phone records off the tower by the store. Might catch the guy up if he used his cell last night in the area. I put all the files on your desk."

"Thanks. Let me know if you find anything."

"Sure. The rookie is in your office putting up the new pictures on the board. He haunts that board ever since he was first on scene and found a victim in the trunk."

"I'll go talk to him."

Dan remembered what it felt like after he found his first victim, but he also remembered how tough his lieutenant was on him. It helped him put it in perspective. Now it was his job to help the "plebe" suck it up.

"Hey, rook."

"Hey, Lieutenant. I added Liza Dean's pictures to the board. Hope you don't mind."

The poor kid looked like he'd lost his best friend.

"Don't mind at all. Good work. How are you doing? You don't look so hot."

"I'm okay, I guess. I never imagined that I would see anything like this when I signed up. As soon as I learned their names, it became personal."

"That's not all bad. Never lose sight of the fact that these victims were someone's child, someone's sister or someone's sweetheart. It has to be personal, but that can't interfere with the way you do your job. It should serve to make you more determined to solve the case. Focus only on that."

"I know." The rookie scanned the evidence board. "It's hard to look at their bodies, though. And even harder to look at him."

He pointed to a still shot of the killer before he had gunned out the garage camera. He turned his head in Danny's direction, a troubled look on his face. "Look at the eyes. It's like looking at pure evil."

The young cop glanced away. Dan noticed the tears in his eyes and was about to deal with the kid's emotionalism when he froze. "That's it. Jesus, rook, you've got something. Eyes. Evil."

Danny closed his eyes and searched his memory for where he had heard those words before. He slapped his hands on his metal desk, sent papers flying and startled the young officer.

Heart pounding, Dan grabbed the phone receiver off his desk and hammered the familiar numbers on the keypad like a man possessed. The young officer left in a hurry.

"Hi, Mom. It's Dan. Is Dad there?"

"He sure is. How are you, Danny?"

"Can I talk to Dad, please? It's important."

"JOHN! Danny's on the phone. You never have

152

time for me, I'm afraid."

Couldn't miss the accusation in his mother's voice. "Not true, Ma. I always have time for you, but this is really important."

"Nothing's more important than talking to your mother while you can. You'll miss me when I'm gone, Daniel."

"You're right. Nothing is more important than talking to my mother. Except this. I really need to talk with Dad."

"He's coming. Did you invite Molly to join us all for Christmas dinner?"

"Yes, I do plan on bringing Molly to Kay's for Christmas...assuming she's free. Is Dad coming to the phone now?"

"I said he was. So are you going to propose to Molly?"

"Not sure, Mom. Yes, maybe there will be a wedding in the future. Where's Dad?"

"He's right here. Was that so hard to be civil to your mother who loves you?"

"No, it wasn't hard to be civil to my mother. I love you, too."

He waited while his mother turned the phone over to his Dad. The brief conversation with her made him feel like he'd run a marathon.

"Hi, Danny."

At last. "Pops. I need your help. You've been following the HH Killer case in the press, right?"

"Sure."

"Anything beyond that?"

"No, why?"

"Let me fill you in."

Danny described the similarities of the victims' slashes and admitted his old habit of eavesdropping on his parents' dinner conversations when he was a little boy.

"I remember one night you told Ma that you

looked into the eyes of evil. Do you remember that case?"

"Never forgot it to this day."

"I knew it."

"The kid was a human skeleton," John Sullivan said.

Dan grabbed a pad of paper from under a stack of files and scribbled notes as his father talked.

"He was about eight years old, but he was so small, he looked five. He had dead eyes and no remorse whatsoever. Killed his father and his mother both. Pure evil. He was institutionalized...criminally insane. I'm sure the records were sealed because he was a minor. But he was at Cascade in southern Illinois. Never forgot that kid."

"Did his mother have red hair?"

"Sure as hell did. Damn. I've never made the connection. You think it's him?"

"Yeah, I do. Thanks, Pops. I think we've made this guy."

Dan dialed information as soon as he disconnected with his father and got the number for Cascade.

A half hour later he had been transferred from department to department and was mired in a bureaucratic maze. He persevered and it paid off. Just when he thought he'd have to get a judge involved, he encountered a talkative employee who'd been around long enough to remember the case.

He slammed down the phone and flew out of his office. He had the evil-eyed kid's name.

Nick looked up from his mound of paperwork.

"Got something?"

"Maybe. Run this name through the DMV system, will you?" He handed Nick a slip of paper.

"Sure." Nick tapped on the computer keyboard.

"Got a hit?" Dan leaned over Nick's shoulder.

"Yep. Arbor Village. 2292 Sycamore."

"You've got to be shitting me? Arbor Village?" Dan headed back to his office and shrugged into his jacket. "Where's Joe?"

"He left a few minutes ago. Said he had a hot date."

"No, I mean my brother, Joe."

"Very funny, Sir."

"I'll give him a call on my way. I'm heading in his direction. If he calls in, let him know I'm looking for him. Barnes, you're with me." Danny tapped the detective on the back.

Barnes grabbed his coat and followed him. "Who is this guy, Danny?"

"Fucking HH Killer if I'm right."

****

The line of customers at the Whole Foods register and the clerk's sunny politeness made Bobbie antsy with impatience. She didn't care if they bagged the stuff she needed to fix Joe a lavish meal in paper or plastic. She couldn't wait to get out of the store and head to Joe's place to talk with him about her plan.

Groceries stowed in the trunk, she drove and jabbed the buttons on the jeep's radio console until she found a country station playing a Phil Vassar song she knew. She tapped her fingers on the steering wheel and kept rhythm with the beat of the piano.

She glanced at the clock. Not too bad. About twenty minutes late even with the delay at the crowded grocery store. She bounced to the music, hummed, and referred occasionally to the crumpled paper with scribbled directions propped in her lap.

On Thanksgiving Day she had spent time alone with Kay while they washed the overflow of dishes together. Kay talked about her career on the force, its rewards and challenges. After deep soul searching since then, Bobbie made the decision to change her life. Joe would be the first person she told. She wanted to pick his brain. She needed to know what she had to do to enroll in the police academy.

It was essential to have everything mapped out before she shared her decision with Molly. That conversation would be hard to handle. Molly always encouraged her to find her calling, but she'd likely have a stroke when she told her she wanted a career in law enforcement more than anything.

Her cell phone played *Someday My Prince Will Come,* and she laughed while she scrambled to pluck it out of her purse. Amy and Mary spent hours changing all the ring tones in her address book. She laughed harder when she saw the caller was Joe. *Never too young to start a little matchmaking. Hmmm. You could do a lot worse. Joe is definitely a prince, but is he* my *prince?*

"Hey, handsome," she answered.

"Well, I'm flattered," came his sweet baritone. "Hey beautiful. I'm running a little late. I just got in. Where are you?"

"According to the directions you gave me, my ETA is about twenty minutes."

"You've been hanging with us cops so much you're starting to sound like us."

Happy with the notion, she still didn't want to share her intentions with him over the phone. "Roger that."

"I'm going to jump in the shower. I'll leave the door unlocked. You can pull around back. I left my truck on the street so you can use my space."

"Sounds good to me. See you in a little while. Hope you're hungry."

"I'm always hungry. Drive carefully."

"Will do." She smiled as she disconnected.

Good thing she got the extra salmon fillets and

the jumbo shrimp. Walnut apple salad, fresh cheese bread, broiled fish and homemade brownies topped with ice cream should fill him to a nice agreeable level.

Joe seemed interested in her as a person, and maybe as a woman, too. She admired him on many levels and knew he would help her make her new dream real.

Thirty minutes later after she compensated for a few wrong turns, she found Joe's condo complex. It was larger than she had thought and was rimmed by a confusion of tiny streets with clever botanical names. She resisted calling Joe to talk her through the directions. What kind of an impression as a pre-rookie cop would she make on him if she couldn't even find a suburban address? She wanted him to take her seriously.

She found his section and street in the maze of identical-looking clusters and crawled behind the brick-faced buildings searching for his parking space. Hidden under the boughs of a majestic weeping willow, she almost missed the name SULLIVAN spray-painted in white on the asphalt. The delicate branches of the tree grazed a whisper along the roof of her car. She popped the hatch, jumped out of the car and grabbed her grocery bags out of the trunk.

Intending to make only one trip from the car, she looped three bags over her left arm and placed the last bag on the ground to shut and lock the hatch with her free hand. A container of ice cream spilled out of the bag on the ground and she stooped to rearrange it. A pervasive scent of Lily of the Valley filled the air. She loved the smell of that flower, but not such an overpowering dose. Funny, it was late fall, not the time for spring flowers.

Still in a crouch, she grinned at the sound of footsteps and swiveled awkwardly from her stooped

157

position in their direction, assuming Joe had come to help her carry groceries. It took her a critical moment to realize the gloved hands that reached toward her were not Joe's. She had no time to react.

A fog encircled her face and she retched in the cloying scent of Lily of the Valley. He jerked her up by the neck, crushing her back against his hard, heaving chest.

"Don't move, carrot top." The cold blade of a knife pressed against her throat and she gagged on the heavy scent of perfume combined with a rotten smell that seemed to gush from the mouth so close to her cheek. The bags slid off her arm.

Have to focus. Have to get away.

Icy tremors raced down her spine. Her mind blanked in a white sheet of terror. *Have to concentrate. Stay in control. Dear God. Help me. Help me think. Help me please.*

"Please don't hurt me," she begged. She tried to regain some composure and regulate her breathing. But her chest contracted erratically and her heart pounded in her ears.

"Ma, don't plead. You *know* how much I hate it when you plead. I *hate* it."

Bobbie wrapped her mind around the demented words, hoping to use them to her advantage. "What kind of son are you to disobey your mother? Put that knife down, boy. Put it down now."

His muscles quivered and the knife shifted slightly. He still gripped her against his chest, his breath ragged and rancid at the back of her head.

"Mother said *now*. Be a good boy and put that knife down."

The pressure of the blade decreased against her skin allowing her the tiniest opportunity to make a move. She whipped her head back, grazing her neck against the sharp blade. She heard a satisfying crack. He grunted and loosened his hold enough so she could twist her body away from him towards the ground.

His hands fisted in her hair and he dragged her upward. She screamed as the roots of her hair tore away from her scalp. She slumped to the ground.

Chapter 18

Molly handed Amy a long, pale lemon dress dotted with embroidered pink rosebuds. "What do you think of this one?"

"Oh Mom. It's perfect. Can I really have it?"

Molly gestured to the dresses folded over her arm. "Why don't you try all these on, too, and see which one you like best?"

"I just know this is the one. Thank you, Mom."

Amy clutched the frothy dress in her thin arms and hurried to the fitting room. Molly trailed behind. By the time Molly caught up, Amy had shed her jeans and sweatshirt and carefully pulled the dress over her slim hips.

Molly zipped up the back and Amy twirled before the mirror.

"It's the bomb!"

"Is that good or bad?"

"Oh, Mom, you are so funny. It's good. Really good. The best. I can't wait to show it to Mary."

Molly shared Amy's happiness and would forever be grateful to Danny. The Charity Girls held an annual Father-Daughter Dance with a Christmas theme. When Danny overheard Mary make plans with her father to attend the dance, he called Amy and asked if he could be her escort.

Her little baby girl wasn't a baby anymore. Before long the dreaded teenage years would be upon her. She prayed that they would stay friends through the pull-tug of hormones, curfews and straining against boundaries. If not friends, at least they could remain on speaking terms through it all.

Who knew what was in their future? She smiled as Danny's cocky grin came to mind. She wondered if he knew how much his invitation meant to Amy. And to her.

****

Danny and Barnes ran to the car in the station house lot. He instructed Barnes to put out an APB for the suspect's car, punched in Joe's number on his cell, then squealed out of the lot.

He was close. He could feel it in the pit of his stomach. The answering machine launched into play.

"Joe. Pick up…" He paused for seconds, hoping his brother was screening. But got only the recording. "I'm on my way to your complex. We've got a suspect. Wait 'til I get there and we'll go in together. 2292 Sycamore. Sorry if I'm interrupting your hot date." Dan chuckled as he disconnected.

Things were coming together. He would stop the killer. He intended to have Molly in his life every day. Hell, he'd have a daughter, too. He and Molly and Amy would be a family.

Fifteen minutes later Dan and Barnes pulled into Arbor Village. On full alert, Danny tensed as he heard a sound that could have been a scream. He pushed the button to open his window, slammed his foot on the gas and skidded over a curb into the parking lot behind Joe's place.

****

The asphalt abraded Bobbie's palms. She

smelled leaves and earth and the sickening smell of synthetic Lily of the Valley.

He stood over her clutching wads of her hair. "Shut up. Shut up, bitch."

He slashed the knife down and she lurched away from its arc. It caught her across the arm, slicing through her corduroy jacket. A red stain bloomed on the light beige material and her arm hung lifeless at her side. She didn't feel the pain or give in to the unreal terror that coursed through her like an electrical current. She fought, writhed, and blindly kicked the monster that hung over her as adrenaline pumped through her body. Her screams pierced the tranquil, willow-shaded scene.

Pounding feet ignited a spark of hope. If he heard, maybe he'd let her go. Hope flickered and died as he buried his hands deep in her hair again and yanked upward. "I'm going to kill you, you bitch. You're never going to hurt me again, Ma. *Never!*"

"Police. Drop your weapon."

Joe's voice was a lifesaver in a storm. Her attacker froze. She saw the muscles tense in the bulky calf near her face. She kicked out with all her strength and caught the back of his leg with the hard toe of her boot. His animal howl cut through the silence, his knee buckled, but he knotted his hands tighter in her hair. She lay limp on the ground and looked up at the nightmare visage of grayish-yellow teeth and maniacal eyes through the slits of a ski mask.

The knife slashed down again and she twisted to avoid it. The blade sliced her back in a trail of fire. The searing pain stole her breath. Her crazy view of feet and the tailpipe of the jeep spun. She inhaled deeply and used the momentum of exhaling to roll toward the tires of the car. From under the tailgate of the jeep she saw Joe's bare feet in the grass twenty feet away. She screamed with all the breath left in her lungs.

****

The suspect's address was in the building next to Joe's. The sprawling complex was a sleepy place this time of day. All but deserted, it shouldn't have been a place where a woman was screaming. But Danny heard it again, distinct now.

He drew his gun and nodded in Barnes' direction. Barnes had heard it, too. They rolled out of the car, assumed a low crouch along its sides and scanned the macadam-covered area and the peripheral scattering of landscaping.

Movement at the far end of the lot near a jeep with the tailgate open caught Dan's eye. A gunshot exploded. He raced towards the sound.

****

Bobbie heard an explosion and then time stopped. The under-carriage of the car dipped toward her head as the masked maniac's body slammed into the jeep, then slithered soundless to the ground. In the same instant the knife left his hand and sailed through the air toward Joe in slow motion.

Animal-like screams filled Bobbie's ears. Disoriented, she realized she made those hysterical sounds, as Joe lay inert on the ground. A knife protruded from his eye. Her left arm numb, blood dripped off her wrist to the pavement. The contents of her purse had scattered on the ground near where she lay. Her cell phone was next to the killer. She closed her eyes, shimmied close to his reeking body and reached for it.

Pounding. Feet. More feet. Coming toward her.

A shadow blocked out the sun and she whimpered, thinking somehow the killer had been resurrected.

"Bobbie. It's Danny. I've got you, Bobbie. Don't move."

Strong hands pressed down on her body.

"Help him," she whispered. "Please help him."

"We will. We're here. Help is coming."

She slipped into a peaceful, black void.

****

Molly left Amy in the fitting room and took the dress to the cashier. She exchanged oohs and aahs over the delicate dress with the saleswoman. Her trauma pager vibrated in her pocket. Amy walked over as Molly read the text. *KNIFE WOUND TO HEAD, ETA 10 MIN.*

"Honey we have to go to the hospital. I'll call Bobbie on the way and she can pick you up there."

"Okay, Mom. I have my backpack with me so I can start my homework and wait for her."

They hurried out of the store to the tiered parking lot. Molly dialed Bobbie's cell phone number as they walked. Frustrated when she got a recording, she left a quick message, and then called the hospital.

"This is Dr. Jordan. I'm on my way in. Should be there in five minutes."

"I'll tell Dr. Kramer," the receptionist replied.

Molly steered down the garage exit ramp. "Why's Kramer involved? My pager referenced a head injury."

"The dispatch from EMS said a knife is imbedded in the eye socket. Kramer's on the trauma team. Neurosurgeon's on call. Kramer picked an ophthalmologist to take over for him in case there isn't other tissue injury to Detective Sullivan's face."

She gasped and her lungs deflated so rapidly that she had to gulp air to keep breathing. Her heart pounded in her ears and her arms shook violently. She fought to maintain enough control to not wail in terror and to ease the car to the curb. Amy's stricken look was enough to snap her to some semblance of professional objectivity.

She accelerated away from the curb and gave a consoling pat to Amy's leg. Her mouth dry as cotton, she gulped. She didn't fully see the road she drove on. Loud voices came through her earpiece. "What's that commotion I hear?"

"You wouldn't believe this circus. We had to call in extra security to manage the press."

"The press? Why?"

"You haven't heard? Sullivan shot the Henna Housewife Killer and saved the victim. She's a level one, multiple knife wounds, and unconscious with substantial blood loss. She'll be here any minute, too."

"I'm almost there," Molly said.

She disconnected and tried to control her breathing. She felt cold everywhere as if terror had turned her to a block of ice. Dr. Brandon Kramer was the best oculoplastic surgeon in the country. If he had a neurosurgeon on call, there might be injury to Danny's brain. *Dear God. Help him. Please save him.*

They turned into the doctor's parking lot and the sound of sirens neared. They sprinted to the bay, Molly relieved to see her team assembled and ready. Without a word Trudy put her arm around Amy and led her off.

She walked toward Dr. Kramer. "What do you we have, Brandon?"

"One twenty to thirty-year-old female. Deep knife wounds to back and arm, head trauma from a fall with major loss of blood from wounds. One thirty to forty-year-old male, unconscious, with knife wound to eye, knife still in the eye area, with possible brain injury. Female's vitals weak but stable, male's vitals erratic."

The twin ambulances screeched into the bay, sirens muted. Lights bounced eerily off the brick façade.

Molly had confidence in her team. They would stabilize Danny and Brandon Kramer would do his job. She couldn't doubt it. She would fly apart if she did.

Doors flew open and Danny's stretcher was hurled out and through the ER doors, phalanxes of doctors, nurses and paramedics on either side. Molly let Danny's stretcher pass and waited for the victim to be lifted down from the truck. Danny was in Kramer's hands. She couldn't run the trauma team to treat him. She was too close to him. She relegated herself to his support team. *How can this be happening? Why is the man I love in jeopardy? Again.*

She would take the lead position on the female victim's trauma team. She prepared to jog next to her stretcher as the paramedics unfolded its legs and set the wheels on the ground. Molly saw the tangled red hair, still pretty despite dirt and twigs knotted in long tendrils, dangle over the side of the stretcher.

She knew before she saw the sweet familiar face. "Bobbie? Bobbie!" She was at the brink of madness in that waking nightmare.

Bobbie blinked open terror-filled eyes and tugged on the oxygen mask that covered her mouth. "Oh, Molly. Please help Joe," she whispered.

"Don't talk, sweetie. Of course I'll help Joe. Where is he? What happened to him?" Molly grasped Bobbie's hand and ran alongside the stretcher on rubber legs.

"Oh my God." Tears trailed down Bobbie's cheeks. "His eye. You have to get it out. Please get the knife out."

Blessed relief and gratitude flooded Molly's senses as she realized Joe was the injured detective, not Danny. The guilt for that selfish reaction would come later. "I promise we'll take good care of you and Joe, sweetie."

166

Molly stepped back and let another attending physician take her place. Bobbie was strong and Molly knew she'd survive. That belief and the knowledge that Joe was in the other room ended the quaking insanity she experienced moments before. A perfect calm settled over her. She knew what she had to do. She realized the exorbitant price she'd pay for the decision but it was necessary for her ultimate survival.

****

Molly felt the adrenaline dissipate with each visit to Trauma Rooms 1 and 2 where Bobbie and Joe were stabilized. When both were wheeled to surgery, she sat on a plastic chair behind the main ER desk. The reality of the past hour punched her in the chest and once again she gasped for breath.

The ER was overrun with blue uniforms. The cops lounged against the walls and flirted with nurses while they waited to gain access to Joe. There was a congratulatory air about them. The members of the press were kept at bay outside the hospital with the promise that a statement about the condition of the officer and the last victim of the Henna Housewife Killer would be provided by an Attending Physician. It was Molly's job to issue the hospital's statement. She'd wait until she could speak with the surgeons before going public about their condition.

She slumped in the chair, eyes closed. Her head spun.

"Molly?"

She lifted her head. "Hi, Trudy."

"Amy's with the Sullivan family in the doctor's lounge on three. Thought you'd want to head up there after you talk to the press."

"Yes. Thanks. I'll do that." She rubbed her eyes. "Do me a favor, okay?"

"Sure."

167

"Tell them I'll be out to give an official statement as soon as both patients are out of surgery. Don't field any questions for now."

"No problem. You look pale. Are you okay?"

"I'm fine."

Determined, she strode down the long corridor to the elevator bank oblivious to the questions from the policemen she passed. She'd encounter Danny with the rest of the family. Would she be able to follow through? Would those bedroom eyes and his cocky grin sway her? She pushed the silver button that would bring her closer to Dan and her decision.

She rode the elevator lost in a fugue state.

You know you have to do this, Dr. Jordan. Take the scalpel. Make the incision. Careful, Dr. Jordan, you have to use steady hands. Fine job. Now laser through the breastbone. Perfect. Pull it apart and ah...there it is, Dr. Jordan. The heart. Now, Dr. Jordan, continue with your plan. Take your heart in your hands. And break it...

I'm ready. I can do this.

Through the glass she saw the family she was already so fond of in the lounge. A few hours ago she had dreams to become part of this close-knit family. The matriarch sat with her rosary beads, her eyes closed in silent prayer. The frustrated patriarch paced. The sister she dreamed Kay would be for her bent in conversation with the girls, no doubt calming their fears. The brothers were all so alike, yet so different. One thing they had in common was a look of fierce solidarity on their handsome faces. "*How dare this happen to my brother?*" they said with their stoic expressions.

Her eyes sought out and settled on the man who had touched her soul. He sat next to his beloved mother, bobbing his leg with each tap of his foot. Hands clenched in fists, he stared at the floor. He raised his head and saw her. She read the stark pain and desperation in their depths.

He sprung from his seat and bolted out the door. "I'm so sorry about Bobbie. I'll never forgive myself for not protecting them. I was too late. I failed them."

"Don't be crazy. None of this is your fault."

"I should have caught the bastard sooner. None of this would have happened."

"They're both going to survive. That's all that matters now."

"I know, I know. We've been getting updates about Joe through Mike but we haven't heard anything about Bobbie. How is she?"

"She should be in recovery soon."

"How are you doing?" He stepped closer and tried to wrap her in his arms.

If she allowed herself she would dissolve there, her hours of terror forgotten. But she wouldn't allow that.

"I'm fine. This is my job. I'm trained to handle these situations."

"These situations? You're kidding, right? This must be killing you to see Bobbie like this."

"You really don't know me at all. I handle these emergencies every day. Bobbie will be fine in a few weeks. Joe will learn to live with his disability."

"Stop one minute. Listen to yourself. These are the people we love that you're talking about with as much emotion as if you were reading a phone book. Where is my Molly? My caring, loving Molly?"

"She's gone. The moment the stretcher carrying Detective Sullivan was wheeled through the ambulance bay doors, she disappeared. I'm ashamed to tell you how relieved I was when Bobbie told me that Joe was injured and not you. I thought it was you. Dear God." Her voice rose and cracked. Tears dotted her lashes. "I knew that minute that it's over for us."

"Don't say this, Molly. You're upset." Again, he tried to hold her but she pulled away. "Please, Molly, don't do this. How can you make any decisions about us now?"

"I'm sorry, Dan. I knew that I shouldn't get involved with you from the beginning. I kept telling myself not to fall for you no matter how attracted I was to you. I went against my better judgment. I'd rather lose you now, a nice clean cut, than spend every day waiting for your stretcher to pull in to my bay."

"Molly, you're being irrational."

"That's where you're wrong. I've never been more rational."

Dan stood silent when Amy ran out the door into Molly's arms. "Mom. How is Uncle Joe? How is Bobbie?" Tears spilled over her freckled cheeks.

Molly held Amy close and felt the shudders ripple through her small body. "They're both going to be okay, honey. They were both very lucky. We'll be able to be with Bobbie in a little while. She's going to need us to take care of her. I hope I can count on you to be strong and help me take care of her."

"I will, Mom. I promise."

"Let's go get your books and see if she's in recovery yet." She steered Amy toward the door of the lounge.

"Molly?" Danny touched her elbow. "What about our conversation?"

"Our conversation is over. Goodbye, Dan."

"I'm not going to say goodbye to you, Molly."

"Have it your way. Let's go Amy."

It took more strength than she'd ever had to muster not to look back at him. The blaze of his temper blistered her back. There would be plenty of time to mourn the loss of love's possibilities. How could any loss compare to what she had suffered when Eddie died? She would protect herself and her daughter so they never hurt that way again. A fracture tore through her chest as the elevator doors closed behind them.

Chapter 19

How does Bobbie do it? Molly dumped the bulky cardboard box on the living room floor, sending up a powdery whoosh of dust in her face. She belatedly thought about possible damage to the ornaments inside it and plopped down into a plush chair.

The silk upholstery felt cool against her overheated body. She was achy and grimy after hauling her huge collection of Christmas decorations up from the basement in installments. The repeat trips from there to the living room, coupled with almost as many ups and downs to the second floor to check on Bobbie, exhausted her and she hadn't even begun decorating.

Waiting for her body to catch up with her mind, she was dead set on infusing some Christmas spirit into her home. Maybe decorating every room would help instill enjoyment of the season in her heart. She doubted it. But she was determined to create a festive environment for Bobbie's recuperation and Amy's innocent delight.

Burning logs crackled in the hearth and cast a flickering golden patina on the dog-eared cardboard boxes. John Denver and the Muppets belted out holiday songs from stereo speakers around the house. Amy was in the family room unpacking her snow globe collection that would cover every inch of the coffee table when she was finished. She heard Amy's pure bell-like voice blend with John's soprano and a gravelly voiced Muppet in a rendition of "The Twelve Days of Christmas". She smiled. *Maybe I'll suggest choral singing to Amy. And I have to give Bobbie a raise.*

She decided to assemble the artificial tree first and have that out of the way. Thank God the lights were built in. If she had to string lights, it might have sabotaged her tenuous Kris Kringle intentions. Truth was she just couldn't seem to care about holiday anticipation or anything else lately.

She set to work, hoping the mindless manual labor would blank her brain. But she kept hearing Danny tell her he wouldn't say good-bye. A chill ran through her remembering her coldness to him. It had to be done despite the price that she continued to pay for the decision.

The phone rang and Amy ran to answer it.

"Mom! Mrs. Lynch is on the phone!" Amy hollered.

She wiped her hands on the sides of her jeans and took the portable phone.

"Hi, Kay. How are you? How's Joe?"

"I'm crazy as usual and still barfing every morning. Who says morning sickness only lasts through the first trimester? Or even the second." She huffed a breathy laugh. "Joe's...as well as can be expected, I guess. Thanks for asking. How's Bobbie doing?"

"Remarkably well. I borrowed on next year's vacation time to ride herd on her. She's hard to keep down. Her wounds are healing but I still won't let her do anything other than use the stairs once a day. I have a new appreciation for all she does for me. I'm putting up the tree for the first time in years. It usually appears like magic every year at the end of a December work day, thanks to Bobbie."

Kay laughed. "I'm so glad to hear she's on the mend. Christmas is the reason I'm calling. Your brood is invited to join us Christmas Eve. Please come. I hope Bobbie is up to it."

Molly's mind raced in a war of opposing desires. She was tempted to see Danny again as much as she wanted to avoid him and protect her heart. She took another dose of her own medicine. "I plan on a quiet holiday here. But thanks so much for the invitation. How about I have your kids for a sleepover New Years Eve? You and Mike can have the evening to yourselves." *That's what I need. I'll be too busy to think.*

"Wow. Sure. Thanks, Molly."

Uncomfortable silence. Molly knew what would come next and she tried to circumvent it. "Listen, I've got to run Kay..."

"Molly? About Danny? Maybe you..."

"Sorry to cut this short, Kay, but Bobbie's calling me. If I don't see you before, Merry Christmas."

She disconnected. She snapped her fingers three times to punctuate the command she recited under her breath like a litany, "Focus, focus, focus."

"Mom?" Amy looked at her like she was crazy. Small wonder.

"Nothing, honey. Gosh you have so many snow globes now. I'll spritz some Windex on a paper towel for you so you can make them shine."

"Thanks, Mom. Will you help me with my hair later?"

"Suuure..." Her mind had been so addled lately she had no idea why Amy would care what her hair looked like on a weekend. "Why?"

"For the dance tonight, Mom. I have to be ready by six." Amy looked at her like she was certain of her craziness. Couldn't blame the kid. "Did you forget?" Amy's voice caught on a plaintive pitch.

"No, of course not." She forced a smile. "I can't wait to see you in your dress. I have to hurry and finish the decorating. I'd love to take your picture under the tree."

She could pretend that the reason she decorated like a mad woman was to have a splendid photographic setting for Amy's special night. She could also pretend that she showered, changed into a sapphire cashmere lounging outfit, and did her hair and makeup so she could look nice in a photo with Amy that Bobbie might agree to take. She could even pretend that she baked two loaves of Kay's luscious pumpkin bread while Amy dressed to give Bobbie a treat. But she knew that she was really preparing for Danny's visit.

He arrived at five to six and Bobbie, who had made her once daily trip downstairs earlier, answered the door. Molly heard their voices and snippets of conversation drift up to her in Amy's second floor bedroom where she helped her little girl finalize her preparations for the dance.

"…you look fantastic. How are you feeling?"

The sound of his voice made her stomach cramp with tension and her nerve endings fire with longing.

"…better. Sick of lying…"

They laughed together and Molly longed to be in on the joke and see his face light with his smile.

"…tree….great…"

"Molly…napping…"

Amy twirled in front of her. "How do I look, Mom?"

She sat on Amy's bed, bowed her head and sobbed in soundless, nose-running heaves.

"Mom, oh my gosh!" Amy threw her arms around Molly's shoulders. "Why are you sad?"

"Oh, sweetie." She grabbed a tissue off Amy's bedside table and blew her nose. "I'm not sad. You look so beautiful. These are happy tears," she lied.

"You go ahead downstairs and greet Uncle Danny. I'll get the camera and be right down."

She took several deep, shaky breaths and leaned toward the mirror over Amy's dresser to assess the damage to her makeup. She spit on her fingers to scrub away mascara smudges and went into the hall. She waited just beyond the open area of the railing, vigilant to hear Danny's reaction to Amy.

"Missy M, you are a vision. You look like a fairy princess. Come down here and let us look at you." He said in a booming voice.

She counted sixteen footsteps on the stairs and knew Amy had reached the bottom of the massive staircase. She envisioned her lovely girl twirling in the foyer in a flower-dotted, lemon cloud of tulle for the appreciative audience of her second mother and stand-in father.

"You look like a porcelain doll," he said. "I have something for you."

Molly walked forward and looked down the stairs. Danny poised on one knee and slid a delicate wristlet of pink rosebuds over Amy's hand. She almost surrendered to messy sobs again when Amy threw her arms around Danny's neck, closed her eyes and leaned in to hug him.

He looked up and saw her. His smile extinguished and his face slackened into a passive mask, except for the stubborn set of his jaw. He stood, six foot four of magnificence in a tuxedo that fit his muscled body to perfection. His mane of black hair was almost tamed with styling gel. His flinty green eyes never left hers as she descended, determined to resist the urge to hop down the stairs and fly to him.

She smiled, the pleasant hostess and greeted

him, "Hello Danny. You look very nice tonight." Her face rubbery, she fought to pinch it into a serene expression.

He didn't return the smile and barely returned the greeting. "Hi."

Amy had fetched a boutonnière—a yellow rose—where it came from Molly had no idea. He bent down, patient, so that the little girl could pin it on his lapel. Amy looked at the straight pin in her one hand and the green florist tape around the rose's stem in her other hand as if they were indecipherable puzzles.

She turned toward Molly. "Mom, I don't know how to work this. Can you help me?" she pleaded.

Molly took the flower from Amy and turned toward Danny. She moved closer to him. He stood rigid, unblinking, and looked straight ahead while she pinned it on his lapel. She smelled the clean, unmistakable scent that was his alone and wanted to bury her nose in his neck. The back of her hand brushed his immaculate white shirt and she thought she felt his heart skip as hers did. He moved a backward step and forced her to let the thick material of his suit jacket pass through her fingers. She didn't know what to do with her hands. She let them fall awkwardly at her sides. He didn't or wouldn't make eye contact with her.

Instead he looked at Amy and smiled. "Let's go to the ball, princess."

They were about to leave when Molly remembered the camera in her pocket. "What am I thinking?" She tapped her forehead with her palm and felt foolish for the gesture. She wanted somehow to connect with Danny and he couldn't be further away. "Can I get a couple of pictures here by the tree before you go?"

Danny acquiesced and produced perfunctory smiles for the camera. Molly's heart broke by

177

fractions with each snap of the shutter that caught the coolness towards her on film.

He took the camera out of her hand and she rode a swell of temptation to grab hold of him when he was within her reach. He moved away smoothly. "Let's get a shot with your Mom, Amy," he directed.

Next Bobbie stepped into the frame. He composed the shot and the shutter clicked. He never hinted to Molly that he was moved in any way by what he saw through the viewfinder.

They left before he said another word to Molly besides his paltry, "Hi."

Molly shut the door behind them, leaned against the carved cherry panel and gave in to the wrenching sobs that had threatened all the while she had been in Danny's stoic presence.

"Oh, Mol, honey." Bobbie wrapped her arms around her. "What's going on with you and Danny? Things were going so well. Don't tell me I have something to do with this."

"No, of course not. All of this is my fault. I broke it off with Danny when you and Joe were injured. I thought…" Another sob took her breath. "I thought Joe was Danny at first. It devastated me. I could hardly breathe. I couldn't bear the thought of losing him like I lost Eddie. Then, when things sorted out, I thought it was clear that I had to end this…to end us…before it went too far."

She dropped her head on Bobbie's shoulder and gave in to her self-created misery.

Bobbie cooed and stroked her hair until the spasms stopped and she was cried out.

"You shouldn't do this to yourself, Molly," she said. "You're in love with him. And unless I'm blind, he's in love with you, too. There's no reason you can't be together."

"I can't go through what I did with Eddie, Bobbie. I just can't." They walked together into the living room and took seats by the fire.

Molly stared at the tree covered with tiny white star lights and dated ornaments that commemorated events in her life before, during and after Eddie. Cold despite the warmth from the hearth, nothing made sense to her. The grief she felt without Danny in her life was just as debilitating as any she had suffered after Eddie's death. Maybe it was worse. Unlike her futile wish to be with Eddie again, she could be with Danny if she let herself - if he would let her.

She glanced over at Bobbie whose head bobbled as she slept in the chair. She roused her, helped her up to bed and tucked her in. Before she left Bobbie's room, she made sure she had the TV remote control, a stash of magazines and books, and fresh water at her bedside.

She wandered back downstairs and flipped channels until she landed on a showing of "White Christmas" in progress. She nestled in the leather sofa, wrapped in an Irish knit afghan, to wait for Amy's return. She had to talk with Danny. At least she had to apologize.

She would offer him coffee and some pumpkin bread, or even a glass of wine or beer. She would tell him that she missed him. Maybe he would agree that he missed her, too. And if he did, maybe there would be a way to be together.

She ate a half pint of chocolate-cherry, cheesecake ice cream, most of a bag of M&M peanuts and a handful of jellybeans. Her nose felt congested from crying and her stomach ached from the pig-out. She was almost glad that she had a physical explanation for what ailed her.

In a sugar-induced doze, she thought she heard the rumble of a car engine. A few minutes later the front door opened and shut. Then Amy was upon her on the sofa, all hugs and chatters about the terrific food and music and how great a dancer Uncle Danny was.

"Where is Uncle Danny? Didn't you invite him in?"

"Yeah, I did, but he said he'd just watch me until I was inside and closed the door." She shrugged. "Did you want to talk to him or anything?"

"No. No. I just thought he might want to visit a while, that's all." Molly held Amy's hand and watched the TV screen cast a blur of colors and motion that didn't penetrate the fog of depression.

"Mom, aren't you going to marry Uncle Danny?"

Molly jolted and stared at her open-mouthed. "Whatever gave you that idea?"

"Mary said you might. And I thought I could tell…"

"Dear God, tell *what?* I didn't know you and Mary talked about these things."

"Well you know…" she hesitated. "The way he looks at you and all. It's the way Daddy looked at you in the pictures."

She turned her head and stared at the TV again. "Oh Amy." She didn't want her to see the hot tears that stung the corners of her eyes. "Well, Uncle Danny isn't like Daddy."

He isn't. The impact of that knowledge made her breath catch and her heart flip-flop. *That will give me something to think about all night.*

Chapter 20

Danny had monumental will power. It took all of it to look and not touch when he had seen Molly descend the stairs and she looked like a fairy princess just as much as Amy. But she had said good-bye at the hospital, plain and simple. There was no masking the finality. He was too proud to beg her to reconsider. However, the sight of her beneath the Christmas tree, all huge eyes and softness, unnerved him and he'd wanted to forget his pride.

Life the past two weeks had been a series of gnawing aggravations and constant self-questioning. He had to do the job of two detectives covering Joe's desk while he recuperated. The guilt he experienced over his brother's injury faded by degrees after each pep talk from both Sullivan women. He couldn't have foreseen the circumstances leading to Bobbie's attack or understood the scrap of information he had on the HH Killer from the only victim he interviewed prior to Bobbie.

Now he knew that Liza Dean was trying to say the word "flower" before she died. Bobbie told him about the blinding cloud of Lily of the Valley perfume sprayed in her face during the attack. It

181

had to relate to the killer's apparent mother-obsession from all the abuse he received as a child. The HH Killer killed his father and then his mother when he was eight years old. Just like he killed twenty-five years later. Those were the facts. Why did he begin killing again? What triggered it? Why not before then? The reasons died when Joe put a bullet in his brain.

Even if he had figured out what Liza said before her life ended, it wasn't enough to go on. That he couldn't get a step ahead of the lunatic and consult his father earlier still plagued him and made him feel responsible for Joe's disability.

"Get straight about this," Kay had demanded. "Joe needs you to stop looking at him with guilt-stricken sympathy. He's looked up to you since he learned how to walk. If you're strong, he'll be strong."

Nobody in the family mentioned that Joe's career was all but ended when he took down the HH Killer. Nobody mentioned Doctor Molly Jordan, either.

With Christmas looming, his estrangement from the woman ate at him unabated like a throbbing abscess. Only weeks before, he had contemplated buying Molly a diamond ring. He thought their joyous lovemaking meant something. He thought he found in her the fierce loyalty and true heart of his life partner. Acting as a surrogate father to Amy for just one night made him continue to fantasize about having the family he hoped for before his marriage splintered. He loved Molly Jordan with the sure knowledge they were meant to be together. He had never been so frustrated and heartsick in his life.

Weary of his constant internal monologue he was itchy for action. He drove the Hummer towards Joe's condo intent on doing for Joe what he couldn't do for himself—give him hope.

A thin snow fell and spotted his windshield with lacy star-flakes. The temperature hovered just above freezing and the snow melted on impact with stubby, straw-like grass and sooty macadam. He had his radio tuned to an oldies station and half-heard the refrain, "How do I live without you? I want to know? How do I ever, ever survive? How do I live?"

"Shit." He punched the off button and drove, his mind as fuzzy as the snow's swirl around the forward motion of the truck.

He got to Joe's and waited, impatient, at his door and squelched the urge to pound on it with his fists when his brother didn't answer immediately. Joe had refused to give a key to any member of the family, even Mom. He wanted his privacy and insisted he was *fine*.

The man who answered the door was a thinner, more wan version of his former self, but Joe was well groomed. He wore pressed gray slacks and a crisp cotton long-sleeved pinstripe shirt, neatly tucked in. He ushered Danny into his home.

As expected there wasn't a speck of dust or clutter anywhere. Danny knew without looking that Joe's bed was neatly made and there were no dishes in the sink. The Sullivan kids learned the commandments of cleanliness from Jean Sullivan. You'd have to be half dead before you broke a single one of them without consequences. As an adult, Joe took his mother's admonitions to heart more than the rest of her brood.

The sight of Joe and his ship-shape house loosened the lump in Danny's throat somewhat. But the thick bandage taped over his eye socket might as well have been a crystal ball foretelling that his brave brother's life would never be the same.

He grabbed Joe, right hand to right hand, and pulled him into a hug. "You're looking good, Joe."

He stepped back and looked into Joe's pastel

blue eye, careful not to avert his eyes or send pity signals in any way.

"Why don't you change into sweats?" he suggested. "I'm in the mood for a little b-ball. The snow's not sticking. We can go over to the hoops at the park off Main Street. I'll beat your ass."

Danny thought he saw a flash of challenge in Joe's eye, but it faded and made him think he was mistaken.

"Nah," Joe said, resigned. "Doctors say I should take it easy. No heavy lifting or anything."

"We're not going build the court. Just toss a ball into the hoop. Besides, who cares what the doctors say? You need some fresh air and exercise."

Danny watched the slow, sly grin bloom on Joe's face. Since they were little Danny was the ringleader and could always talk his brother into ignoring the rules. He gave him a complicit wink and lounged on the sofa while Joe changed.

Danny drove to the court, which was deserted and looked forlorn in the winter gloom. They lumbered companionably toward the hoop, two tall, physically fit men in cut-off sweats and thin bright-colored shirts. They could dominate a playing field, an appreciative woman, any comers and the very season of winter itself.

Danny bounced the ball with lazy control, spinning it down with careless flicks of his huge palm. He picked up speed, bounded to the hoop, launched a pretty decent five feet off the ground and arced one ball-carrying arm into an effortless lay-up. He caught the ball on the swish down and sent it towards Joe's midriff with a powerful sweep.

He caught it easily and dribbled it, a thoughtful expression on his face. "I'm not up for one-on-one. Let's play 'horse.'" He sunk a one-handed, three-pointer.

"Wuss," Danny teased. He moved to Joe's

position, shot and missed. His excuse, which he wouldn't voice, he was weak with relief that Joe passed his improvised reflex test.

"Ha! Who's the wuss? Try this one." Joe dribbled the ball side to side under each leg, twisted and sprung to the hoop for a passable stuff and a nice hoop hang.

They were soaked with sweat when Danny was declared the "horse." He was out ten bucks and more than a modicum of pride. He didn't let his injured brother beat him, either. He was both grateful and pissed he didn't have to artificially boost Joe's ego.

They showered at Joe's place and ordered delivery of assorted Chinese food from the Golden Wok. They ate the meal in front of a fifty-inch plasma screen; techno-gadgets being Joe's weakness. They watched the Bears play the Vikings in brilliant, eye popping high definition. The hues of the players' jerseys vibrated in cobalt, gold, orange and white against the turf, such a perfect shade of green it looked unearthly. The silence between them comfortable, only occasionally broken by some epithet tossed at an ump or player.

At a commercial, Joe picked up his plate and held his hand out for Danny's. "Want a beer?"

"Sure. I'll get us each one." Danny followed Joe in to the kitchen.

"Think I can get certified active again?" Joe asked over the rush and clatter of rinsing the dishes at the sink.

Danny froze, his arm over the refrigerator door, and stared at a container of orange juice on the interior rack. He'd been dreading this question from Joe and didn't want to squash what little enjoyment he had from winning their match earlier. But he never lied to Joe and he wouldn't start now.

"Improbable, but not impossible. The captain put in for a medal for you. You're a bona fide hero and you deserve it. You'll always have a job on the force, you know."

Joe nodded. His expression told Dan nothing. He caught the beer Dan tossed him and they returned to the game.

"How's Bobbie?" Dan asked later.

"Don't know." Joe took a swig of beer and stared at the TV. "How's Molly?"

"Don't know," Dan replied.

****

Christmas came and the Sullivan clan assembled—a bunch of stag brothers in their married sister's house who borrowed her family life and played Santa to her kids. It was fun like it had always been in years past, but minus Molly, Amy and Bobbie, a sorry comparison to Thanksgiving Day in Dan's brooding opinion—an opinion which he kept to himself.

Then it was New Year's Day, then the January doldrums. Snow fell, temperatures dropped and the Chicago winds swept the frozen ground in vaporous gusts. The ground hog cast his shadow, which never mattered anyway. Time passed and did nothing to diminish the pain Dan felt from the loss of Molly.

He saw her in his mind as vividly as if she were there with him whatever he did and wherever he went. He avoided the hospital except to accompany Joe for a check-up. While there, he made sure he didn't run into her. In his heart he longed to see her turn every corner.

She had never been to the station with him, so there he had no specific memories to wrestle. It didn't matter. Even though it never happened before, he wanted to see her walk up to his desk, and maybe sit on it so he could shove papers aside and make wild love to her right there where his job, that she considered so taboo, was done.

He was tired of this painful separation, tired of

the idea that a job prevented him from having what he wanted most. Molly was his woman. He had to have a life with her.

He opened his desk drawer and pulled a wrinkled, letter-sized paper out. He referred to it as he dialed the phone.

Chapter 21

The new owners of Fannie May candy closed every retail store, regrouped and re-launched the candy line in time for Valentines Day. Molly didn't mind standing in line with the crowd that resulted from the pent-up demand. Fannie May chocolates were worth the wait. The store was lit so bright white it hurt her eyes. A young mother at the head of the line, unfazed by the growing numbers of impatient people behind her, explained to the saleswoman the reason her two well-behaved children could have their choice of candy.

"Frank Jr. and Dianne were such angels in the doctor's office this morning. I promised them a treat if they were good and they so deserve it." The slim brunette blew her bangs out of her eyes and transferred a squirming, pointing toddler boy from one boney hip to the other. The little girl, nestled at her side, pointed shyly to the display of foil-covered chocolate hearts.

"We will take a bag of those chocolate hearts and two cherry lollypops," the brunette said.

The plump, gray-haired woman behind the counter smiled, filled a small bag with their goodies and handed it to the little girl.

"Anything else, dear?" she asked to the obvious dismay of the Armani-clad man in front of Molly. He checked his Rolex for the third time. Molly chuckled as the mother took her time in front of the glass-covered display and considered each Valentine heart-shaped box. If Armani-man were behind her instead of in front of her and next in line, Molly wouldn't be cruel enough not to let him go first.

"I'm sure my husband won't remember today is Valentine's Day. I might as well get myself a little something."

The young mother selected a box of candy and juggled her child and purse to complete her purchases. The man behind her tapped his foot, which didn't make the sales transaction happen any faster, but he didn't stop the exasperated tapping until the mother towed her kids out the door.

The woman seemed okay with the probability that her husband would treat February 14th like any other day—amazing. As the man in front of her took his turn, she thought back to the first Valentines Day after she married Eddie.

She had worked hard to make a special dinner for him. She wasn't an accomplished cook, but she was eager to impress him with a "gourmet" meal. One of the nurses gave her an easy recipe for Shrimp Diablo.

The exotic aroma of spices filled her tiny kitchen as the shrimp bubbled in sauce and a pot of salted water boiled ready for her to drop in store-bought-homemade pasta. Eddie came home, gave her a quick kiss, hurried into their bedroom to change out of his uniform and sat down at the table like royalty waiting to be served.

"Something smells good. What's the special occasion?" he said, oblivious to the lit red candles, her red dress and what she thought was the blatant

Valentine motif.

"Aren't you forgetting something?"

"No? What?"

"It's Valentine's Day." She said with an implied, "Duh."

"Oh, that." He leaned back in his chair and continued in a professorial tone. "Honey, it's just another day—an invention of flower growers, candy makers and Hallmark. I don't need a special day to tell you I love you. You know I do."

"You always remembered when we were dating. You know how much I love Valentine's Day." She tried not to whine.

"We're married now, honey. We don't need a senseless holiday."

With her calm doctor's demeanor she picked up the steaming plate of pasta and shrimp that she had just placed in front of her husband and dumped it in the sink.

She was amazed when he belly-laughed, jumped up from the table, and grabbed her in a bear hug. Before she could speak, he planted a deep, lingering kiss on her mouth and led her by the hand to their bedroom.

A lilac-scented candle flickered on her end table that cast soft, dancing lights on a huge, heart shaped box of chocolates on the bed and a red, satin teddy that draped her pillow.

"How could I ever forget my Valentine?" he asked sweetly. "You should know me better than that." He took her hand and pulled her closer to the bed.

"You worked hard on the dinner. I hope you don't mind that I planned the appetizer." He kissed her again, a prelude to a memorable session of nightlong lovemaking and a shrimp dinner literally down the drain.

"May I help you, dear?" Molly blinked away the vivid reverie at the sound of the saleswoman's voice.

"Um, yes. Sorry. I was daydreaming. I'd like a pound each of coconut and raspberry creams. And the Trinidads look so good, I think I'll take a pound of those, too."

She watched the woman weigh her chocolates and place them in individual white boxes.

"Anything else?"

"What the heck. I'll take a pound of the foil hearts, too." She bent down and peered at the neat stack of chocolate treasures in the display case. "Let's see. I need some nuts."

The saleswoman's eyes twinkled with merriment. "We ladies all need our nuts on Valentine's Day."

She snorted at the double entendre. "We ladies certainly do. I'll take a pound of the pixies. Sad to say, the pecans in them will be the only nuts I get this Valentine's Day."

The clerk chuckled and murmured general condolences. Molly hoisted the heavy shopping bag over the counter. "Thanks. You made my day. Hope you get a nice valentine."

A pervasive, gray layer of clouds blanketed the landscape. Blustery gusts of wind whipped her hair into her eyes and threatened to blow the heavy bag out of her grip as she ducked into her car. "Brrrr. Will Spring ever come?" she said to the sky.

While she waited for the car heater to kick in, she stripped foil off one of the hearts and popped it in her mouth. She closed her eyes, let her head fall back on the headrest and savored the creamy, sensual delight that melted on her tongue. She could almost ignore the sunless overcast plied with chocolate.

She was so tired of the bleak weather that matched her moods. If the sun would shine and flowers bloomed again, she might be able to snap out of the funk she was mired in since December. She had managed to limp through the holidays and hoped that Amy never realized how her heart wasn't in the glad tidings and peace on earth. She went through the motions and decorated, wrapped presents and baked way too many cookies. But she felt detached from everyone and everything, like watching her life from a distance. Still did.

Amy stopped mentioning Uncle Danny. Kay, bless her, continued to include Amy in their family celebrations, despite Molly's polite refusal of invitations. At least Amy didn't suffer for the mess she'd made of things with the Sullivan family.

Molly doubted her decision to push Danny away through many sleepless nights. She missed him unbearably at first, but she thought the feeling would fade. She thought wrong. Aching even more because she created her own suffering, she questioned everything.

She'd spend the holiday of lovers alone because she told Danny good-bye. Was her life better? Was grieving the end of their relationship more bearable than the worry she tried to avoid? How long would she continue to live a half-hearted existence? She felt so removed from everything, never quite present in the moment.

She switched on the radio. "How do I live without you?" pleaded LeAnn Rimes' haunting voice. "I want to know? How do I ever, ever survive? How do I live?"

Good question. She pulled into her garage, switched off the ignition and hit the steering wheel flat with her palm. *I need to know. Can he forgive me? Is it too late to ask for a second chance?*

Questions without answers spooled in her head. She went inside and sought out Bobbie. She found her in the family room where she had set everything up for their Valentine pity party.

Votive candles in frosted milk glass holders

192

glimmered in a row atop the mahogany mantle. A fire blazed behind an ornate brass screen. A stack of DVDs, an open bottle of cabernet and two oversized wine glasses were set on the round, marble-topped coffee table. An assortment of cheeses, salamis and crackers completed the feast.

Bobbie, her slim body hidden in two sizes, too big, flannel pajamas, sat with her legs folded lotus style on the floor next to the coffee table. Her copper hair was wound in a loose knot on the top of her head, held by bamboo picks that stuck out like crossbones. She dug inside the shopping bag that Molly dropped on the floor next to her. "Oh yum, my favorite. Pixies! You outdid yourself, Doc."

She tore at a foil-covered heart and deposited pieces of the wrapping in a small pile on the table. "I've been waiting all day for this moment." She tossed the candy into her mouth. "Yes, yes! Almost an orgasm."

Molly stood over her laughing. "Did you drop Amy off at the party?"

"I did. I don't know how Kay does everything she does. She's about to drop the baby any minute and still finds the time and strength to host a Valentine Party for ten little girls. I offered to help but she said the uncles were all going to be there to help. Wouldn't you love to be a fly on the wall to see that?"

A sharp pang of longing to be there with Danny sliced through Molly. "All the uncles?"

"According to Kay, yes, but I can't see Joe going. Word has it he's holed up in his apartment and refuses to see anyone. I know for sure he refuses to see me."

"He just needs a little time. Adjusting can't be easy for him."

"I guess so." Bobbie poured the wine.

Molly took in the wistful expression on Bobbie's face. *This will be the pity party of all pity parties.*

193

"Let me go and get some loose comfortable clothes on so we can pig-out on all this stuff."

She hurried back to join Bobbie after she had shed her work clothes. She wore baggy black sweats torn at both knees and an oversized NYPD gray sweatshirt. She sank into the butter soft couch and tucked her bare feet under her.

She grabbed a glass of wine and fingered its stem. "Okay, Bobbie. I'd like to clear the air. I'm sorry for the way I reacted to your decision to enter the police academy. I've been so stubborn by refusing to discuss it with you and I know I hurt your feelings. I'm very sorry."

"That's okay. I knew you'd oppose the idea of my getting into law enforcement. I don't blame you for your reaction."

Bobbie was too loyal to ever accuse her of unfairness. It made Molly feel guiltier that she had indeed been unfair to her.

"No, it's not okay. I've been distant and unapproachable," Molly admitted. "I love you and I've been wrong to shut you out. I want you to know I support you and I really do want to hear all about your plans. I'm so proud of you. I know you'll be the best police officer."

Bobbie sprang up and hugged Molly who kept one eye on her teetering wine glass.

"You don't know how much this means to me, Molly. I've missed being able to talk to you about anything so much. I know you're afraid, but for the first time in my life I feel like I've found what I've been searching for."

"I can see that and I promise I'll support you one hundred per cent. Eddie would be so proud of you, too."

They wiped their eyes and blew their noses on heart-shaped paper napkins. Together they dove for the chocolate.

Molly sniffed. "I expected to be crying because I had to buy my own Valentine candy."

"We have wine, chocolate, and movies. *We don't need no stinkin' Valentine.*" Bobbie's impersonation of Cheech of Cheech and Chong, dead on.

"So true," Molly agreed. She looked through the stack of movies on the table. "*An Affair to Remember,* I love that movie. Makes me cry every time. *Love Story, Roman Holiday, and Splendor in the Grass, Grease* - all my favorites. *Friday the Thirteenth?* I'm not going to watch that one."

"I had to pick at least one movie for me," Bobbie said. "I don't like those soppy tear-jerkers."

Astonished that Bobbie could bear to watch a horror movie after the nightmare she had lived through in real life, Molly admired her resilience. She could learn a great deal by Bobbie's example. Bobbie was fearless and would do well at the academy.

"You can watch that one by yourself later. I have enough trouble sleeping lately."

They snacked content to be together. Sparks popped in the hearth and firelight reflected through the screen that cast a checkerboard of dim illumination and shadows against the furnishings.

"Did you hear from Joe at all today?" Molly asked, her mouth full.

"No. I hoped he would call but in my heart I knew he wouldn't. I thought we had the start of something. He's funny, caring and gorgeous. I felt so natural when I was with him. He was really easy to talk to. Have you talked to him lately? He doesn't return my calls. When I asked Kay about him she just shook her head and said things weren't good with him. I've tried but he obviously doesn't want to see me."

She aimed a rueful grin at Molly. "He's been through so much because of me, I can't force anything."

"Wait just a minute." Molly tossed a cracker on the plate and leaned toward Bobbie. "You're not the reason he was injured. There was a mad man out there. It was Joe's job to stop him and he did his job. It's terrible that he was badly hurt in the process. But don't carry around guilt for something you couldn't control. You were the victim."

"I know, I know. But I get the feeling Joe is blaming me."

"If he is, it's his problem not yours. You can't control how Joe's feeling, either."

"You're right." Bobbie's face brightened. "Enough about me. Did you hear from Dan at all today?"

"No. I half-hoped he would call or stop in at the hospital. Of course, I knew he wouldn't after the way I treated him. I've been wrong about so many things. My fears have caused me to hurt the people I love. And hurt myself in the process. I need to change. I want to, but I don't know how. Any suggestions?"

"If you want Dan back in your life, go for it. I think you're going to have to take the first step. Those Sullivan men are proud. I don't see Dan calling you."

"I don't see me calling him, either. It's not that I'm too proud, but I think I might have done too much damage and waited too long to apologize. How can I call him up and say, 'Gee, Dan, I'm sorry I was so heartless and rejected you in the waiting room of a hospital while you were sick with worry about your brother. But now I've had a change of heart and I've been miserable for the last two months. How about we try it again and see if I hurt you or not this time?'"

"Well." Bobbie smiled. "I think you might want to rephrase that a little. But essentially you have to tell him how you feel."

Bobbie selected another chocolate and tossed the whole piece in her mouth. "All my teeth ache, but this is so delicious."

She flexed her legs, pushed up from the floor and sat on the couch next to Molly. "I have an idea. Tomorrow is the medal ceremony for Joe. I know you said you didn't want to go, but come with me anyway. I need the moral support and you need to see Dan. After the ceremony I'm sure you'll be able to talk to him. Tell him what you've been feeling. Tell him how much you miss him. Talk from your heart. Make him listen to you."

"I don't know if I can do that."

"Of course you can. You can do anything. You're doctor Molly Jordan who puts Humpty together again. Now that's settled. Let's do some serious damage to this chocolate. Who needs men when you've got Fannie May?"

Chapter 22

Molly regretted that they hadn't taken the train into the city instead of driving Bobbie to the ceremony. Wherever she looked as four rows of traffic inched, tail pipes steamed and engines idled, the world stalled in a monochrome landscape. Late winter slush lined the shoulder of the Eisenhower Expressway like aged remnants of lingering Christmas snow, a former winter wonderland turned sooty gray and dismal. She once teased a colleague from New York that February in Chicago was like having the inside of your eyeballs painted gray.

She sighed and tried not to look at the dashboard clock as her right foot swung from accelerator to brake and the car's sparing progress made her chest tighten with frustration. Her hands clenched the steering wheel as if she could push the car faster with forward tension on the wheel.

"I'll drop you at the curb in front of the hotel and see if they'll valet the car," she said to Bobbie. "If they won't, you go in and I'll park in the theatre lot off Lake Street."

"Okay."

Molly glanced sideways. Bobbie sat tensed next

to her in the over-warm car. A waft of Kate Spade fragrance drifted toward Molly and the floral bouquet of Bobbie's signature perfume soothed her frayed nerves and made her smile.

She laid her hand over Bobbie's and decided to keep it there to infuse some warmth into her friend's icy fingers. "Don't be nervous, sweetie. You'll do fine."

"I'm freaking out." Bobbie turned her palm into Molly's and grasped her hand. "I've never given a speech before. And this? The Mayor will be there. And TV cameras for god-sake. I'm afraid I'll sound like a fool."

"You won't." Molly loosened the handhold and changed lanes as the traffic unclogged after the Kennedy Expressway exit lanes. She sped over the bridge that spanned the ice-lumped Chicago River. The tires whined on slick metal and she turned off the highway and swooped left toward the dip to Lower Wacker Drive.

She drove the rest of the way to The Renaissance Hotel with the abandon of a city cab driver. Twenty minutes before the ceremony was due to begin, she dropped Bobbie off at the hotel and left her car on the level of the theatre district's parking garage marked *Oklahoma*. The refrain from that Broadway tune played through speakers at the elevator bank on her floor and it looped in her brain as she power-walked back to the hotel.

She entered the ballroom with minutes to spare and found an empty seat in the back. The invitation they had received from Francis J. Cargill, Superintendent of Police, highlighted the singular honor of the one-recipient-only award ceremony that day. Usually police commendations and medals were awarded at an annual event in May during National Police Month. But the high-profile nature of the HH Killer merited a special commendation for Joe.

Detective Joseph M. Sullivan would receive the department's highest award, the Police Medal, along with the Superintendent's Award of Valor at a special ceremony just for him. Bobbie, the guest of honor, would have an opportunity to express her gratitude to Joe for saving her life at the cost of grave injury to him.

Molly undid the buttons on her soft alpaca coat with numb fingers and tried to calm down. She rationalized that her racing heart was the after-effect of her athletic pace from the parking garage, and not from tangled memories and Danny's certain presence in the same room.

The sight of what had to be hundreds of officers in Class-A, dress uniforms would inspire awe in any spectator. But for Molly the floodgates of repressed memories opened and threatened to drown her.

Eddie had worn his Class-A uniform, many times after September 11th. Reserved for funerals and awards ceremonies, the uniform paid homage to heroes, fallen and standing. Clad in that handsome uniform, Eddie guarded flag-draped coffins and gave ovations to medal of valor recipients. Then he was decorated himself and others guarded his flag-draped coffin.

Collective conversations from the crowd buzzed in Molly's ears. She reeled, dizzy, when the buzzing continued even after Superintendent Frank Cargill stepped up to the microphone on the dais in front of the ballroom and the crowd quieted.

Behind him a row of officers sat on folding chairs, legs angled to reveal scraps of black sock-covered ankles beneath sharp-creased trousers over mirrored, polished shoes. Their spines straight, their hands rested at ease in their laps. Mustard gold bands circled some jacket cuffs: one for Lieutenant, two for Captain, and three for Police Chief. Brass buttons gleamed in even rows against midnight black worsted wool stretched across hard-bodied torsos. They were a linear blur to Molly who didn't hazard a look at the officers' faces. She was afraid if she met someone's eyes, she'd burst into tears.

Hizzoner, the Mayor, hair mussed and tie knot off-center, flanked Bobbie at the end of the row of chairs that faced the audience. She looked like a perfectly groomed civilian version of the officers to her left. She sat erect, knees pressed together beneath the demure length of her black, wool skirt hem. She wore a matching double-breasted jacket with gold buttons made less military by the fringe of delicate, ivory camisole lace in the vee of her jacket lapels. Molly knew Bobbie wouldn't believe it, but she planned to tell her how beautiful she looked the minute the ceremony was over.

She concentrated on Bobbie's face and sent her a telepathic mantra of support. Her scattered thoughts were so loud inside her head that the superintendent's voice became an indecipherable, amplified reverberation in her ears.

Danny was there somewhere. She felt his presence. She admitted it was the only reason that she came. She didn't have to come. Bobbie, although nervous about her role, didn't really need shepherding. True, Molly wanted to express her gratitude to Joe for saving Bobbie's life.

But she could have chosen a different place to thank Joe where she wouldn't risk a confrontation with Danny. The pain she suffered from their separation was part of the kaleidoscope of upsetting feelings the award ceremony dredged up. Her palms were clammy inside her clenched hands. Feverish and insecure, she prayed for composure.

The Mayor stepped to the mic and she ventured a scan of the audience in search of Kay as the Sullivan family focal point, but couldn't find her. The sea of identical police hats and uniformed backs that

201

stretched before her made it unlikely that she could pick out Danny from behind. Still, if she could watch him without his knowledge she thought it might clear away the confusion she felt in that situation where Eddie and Danny's worlds collided in her mind.

The speaker's words penetrated the hum in her head and she paid attention to his summary of the events that brought them there to honor Joe's bravery. Molly shuddered as her mind conjured up the nightmare Bobbie and Joe dealt with together. The Mayor's public speaking, despite his sometimes-disheveled appearance, was consistently polished, articulate and inspirational. He was in his finest form as he lauded Joe and introduced Bobbie. The audience erupted in enthusiastic applause when he relinquished the mic to Miss Roberta Leighton.

Bobbie looked smaller than her five foot eight inch frame in front of the wall of testosterone behind her. She must have pinpointed Molly's position in the crowd earlier because she trained her eyes directly into Molly's before she spoke.

"Joe Sullivan saved my life. Not just because he took aim and fired a fatal shot into a crazy man who tried to kill me. I took a self-defense class that he taught and he saved my life in a junior college classroom. He taught me to use my head to stave off an attack. When I was attacked his words penetrated the paralyzing terror I felt and helped me act. Without his guidance I wouldn't have lived long enough for Joe to save me with his weapon. I am so sorry that he was badly hurt helping me.

"My employer and best friend, Doctor Molly Jordan, along with her daughter, Amy, have a tradition in our house to wish each other happiness. We learned it from our parish priest out East, Father Chuck Hartling. It's based on a series of wishes.

"I wish you enough sun to keep your attitude bright.

"I wish you enough rain to appreciate the sun more.

"I wish you enough happiness to keep your spirit alive.

"I wish you enough pain so that the smallest joys in life appear much bigger.

"I wish you enough gain to satisfy your wanting.

"I wish you enough loss to appreciate all that you possess.

"I wish you enough hellos to get you through the final good-bye.

"Detective Joseph Michael Sullivan, I thank you from the bottom of my heart. But most of all, I wish you enough."

Bobbie turned and stepped to where Joe sat. She stretched her hand toward him. He stood, a trim black soldier from the neck down, a pirate with a black eye patch from the neck up. He took Bobbie's hand and allowed her tearful embrace, his face impassive over her shoulder.

Bobbie took her seat to thunderous applause and sought out Molly again. Their eyes held and welled with tears. A head turned in the front row of the audience and caught Molly's attention. Black curling hair brushed his jacket collar. Their eyes locked. Her past and present fused as she stared into Danny's piercing green eyes and she knew that she looked into her future. He was the first to break the stare when the superintendent asked the officers in the Sullivan family to join him on the platform.

The father and his five sons stood before them. It was such an impressive sight that the audience applauded again. With his family at his side, Joe smiled. He received his awards and stepped to the microphone. The Sullivan men moved forward with him.

"Thank you, Your Honor Mister Mayor, Superintendent Cargill, my superior officers, colleagues, all the members of my family and friends who are here today. I'm very humbled by this honor and don't feel worthy to receive it. I was in the right place at the right time and I did what any member of my profession would have done. Thank you, Miss Leighton for your words. I, too, am very grateful that you survived.

"A special thanks to my brother, Lieutenant Detective Daniel Sullivan for teaching me everything I know about police work, including what to say at the self-defense course that Miss Leighton referred to earlier. It has been an honor serving in the homicide department with you, Danny, and I wish you every success in your new post at the Police Academy. Those recruits will be lucky to have you for a teacher.

"Thank you everyone for coming today."

Molly clapped her hands along with everyone else but didn't feel their impact against each other or hear the sound they made. She was stunned, lost in Danny's playful stare and the grin that lit his face. Scattered camera flashes ignited like fireflies on a summer lawn and the crowd milled around the ballroom and on the dais.

She stood and stepped forward as he stepped down, magnetized to each other. They maneuvered through the crowd and gathered speed until they crashed into an embrace that pulled her high off the ground with its momentum. She looked down at his upturned face and they smiled, elated, as her body slowly slid down against his chest. Their lips met and she sank greedily into the kiss, her feet still off the ground.

All she had been missing dissolved in the heady moment of reconnecting with the man she wanted forever. He was her anchor. He was her love.

Their lips parted and she slid the rest of the way to the floor. Breathless, she whispered, "You did this for me."

He nodded and pulled her close. "I couldn't let a job keep us apart. I love you, Molly."

"Oh, Danny, I love you, too." She pressed her lips against his neck and settled in the amazing comfort of his arms. For the first time in months she felt connected, unafraid and gloriously alive.

"I had already decided to beg you to be with me. You don't have to change your job for me, Danny. If you want to reconsider..."

He pulled back and looked at her. His eyes, direct as a laser, gleamed with intensity. "The job was posted and I missed you. It was time. Some things are meant. We're meant. I told you I wouldn't say good-bye."

He crooked a finger under her chin and tilted her head up. There was a dangerous glint in his moss green eyes. "Marry me," he demanded.

She cocked her head and challenged him, "Is that an order?"

He didn't smile or change his expression, but his eyes warmed with emotion. "Only if you'll follow it for the rest of your life."

Printed in the United States
125366LV00001B/19/P

9 781601 543509